DATE DUE			
NOV 1 8 1991	DEC 12		
DEC 1 3 1991			
JUN 1 5 1992			
OCT 31 '94			
NOV 22 '94			
12-10-98			
1-8-99			
4-24-99			
JUN 07			
OCT 25			
Jun 18			

Media Center
Willits High School
299 N. Main Street
Willits, CA   95490

Where Are You When I Need You?

Where Are You When I Need You?

BY SUZANNE NEWTON

 VIKING

The author gratefully acknowledges the help received
from a North Carolina Writers Fellowship
jointly supported by a grant from the North Carolina Arts Council
and the National Endowment for the Arts in Washington, D.C.,
a federal agency

VIKING
Published by the Penguin Group
Viking Penguin, a division of Penguin Books USA Inc.,
375 Hudson Street, New York, New York 10014, U.S.A.
Penguin Books Ltd, 27 Wrights Lane, London W8 5TZ, England
Penguin Books Australia Ltd, Ringwood, Victoria, Australia
Penguin Books Canada Ltd, 2801 John Street, Markham, Ontario, Canada L3R 1B4
Penguin Books (N.Z.) Ltd, 182–190 Wairau Road, Auckland 10, New Zealand

Penguin Books Ltd, Registered Offices: Harmondsworth, Middlesex, England

First published in 1991 by Viking Penguin, a division of Penguin Books USA Inc.
1 3 5 7 9 10 8 6 4 2
Copyright © Suzanne Newton, 1991
All rights reserved

Library of Congress Cataloging in Publication Data
Newton, Suzanne.
Where are you when I need you? / by Suzanne Newton.
p. cm.
Summary: When Missy Card wins a college scholarship, she has a hard time deciding
whether or not to leave the security of her small hometown.
ISBN 0-670-81702-3
[1. Universities and colleges—Fiction. 2. Separation anxiety—Fiction.]
I. Title.   PZ7.N4875Wk 1991
[Fic]—dc20 90-42044 CIP AC

Printed in the United States of America
Set in Meridien

For Sonja
The first

Also by Suzanne Newton

M.V. Sexton Speaking
I Will Call It Georgie's Blues
An End To Perfect
A Place Between

Chapter 1

"I broke the news to the family last night," I said.

Ms. Hollins looked up from the papers piled on the desk in front of her. The light from the lamp shone on her brown skin and dangling peacock-feather earrings. She pointed to the leather chair beside the desk. "Well?"

"It was pretty awful," I said, as I came in and sat down. "I don't know if I can hold out."

Her eyes narrowed. "Don't you talk like that, Missy Cord. You're exactly what every college in this country is looking for. Do you want to stay in Tucker forever?"

"No, ma'am, I don't. But I don't like being on one side with my folks lined up against me on the other, either."

Ms. Hollins has a way of not arguing, just looking at you in a challenging way that makes a person have to explain.

"Maybe things would be different if it was just Mama and me," I said. "But what we've got is Uncle Tate, who's bossed women around since he was born, and Gramma, who always thinks men are right. That's a lot for Mama to overcome."

"But what about you?" said Ms. Hollins. "Somehow, I don't see you knuckling under to anyone, Missy. You've had college as your goal ever since ninth grade. Think of the work you've put into it—taking all the college prep courses and the SATs, working afternoons and summers and saving your money, paying the application fees. You want all that to go down the drain?"

I sidestepped the question. "It was having to get Mama to fill out that Financial Aid Form that messed me up. If I'd been able to keep it to myself and not tell anyone till I started out the door next August, everything would've been fine."

Ms. Hollins laughed and leaned back in her chair. "Girl, you couldn't keep something this important a secret forever! It would be like an elephant trying to hide behind a telephone pole. Something's bound to show."

"I knew it would be like this," I said. "College has been a dirty word in our household for as long as I can remember."

"Yes, but that's never stopped you before, has it?"

"No," I admitted. "But I guess I underestimated just how strongly they felt about it."

"It's pretty unusual for someone who wants to go to college not to have their family's blessing," Ms. Hollins said. "Usually it's the other way around. Parents want their kids to go and the kids don't want to."

I wouldn't look directly at her. Ms. Hollins knows that Mama went to college for a couple of years back in the sixties and then came home, but she doesn't know the whole story. I don't either, actually. Somewhere along there is when I was born, and the man who's supposed to be my father, Bill Cord, is never mentioned kindly.

"I'll never get Uncle Tate's blessing," I said, "or Gramma's as long as *he* lives with us. The big problem is seeing that he doesn't bully Mama so much that I can't get hers. If that happens, I don't know what I'll do. I have to have financial aid."

Ms. Hollins leaned forward and folded her hands on the desk. "Would it help if I talked with your mother? Or with your uncle?"

The very thought of Uncle Tate in the same room with Ms. Hollins made me cringe inside. "Maybe not yet," I hedged, getting up to leave. "Thanks, though."

"Well, just don't let anybody talk you out of your plan. If you feel a backslide coming on, you get down here pronto, understand?"

She was already poring over those papers again before I was out the door of the Guidance Office.

By the time I got back to homeroom, the buses had begun to arrive, lumbering into the gravel parking lot like so many orange elephants, with brakes squealing, wheels crunching, and kids hollering out of the half-open windows. Number 78 is the one I usually take. Not many juniors and seniors ride the buses, though. Most have cars of their own. From the second-floor window, I could see

3

the senior parking lot. Right away I spotted Jim Perkins's Ford Ranger pickup truck and Sue Gibbs's little red Honda, those two being the ones I've ridden in most.

Sue is easy to recognize from a distance because of her hair, curly to the point of frizz and so red it looks like it would burn your finger if you touched it. There are things about her that irritate me sometimes, but they're not her fault. Under it all she's a pretty decent person. It's her pushy mother who's always trying to make her into some kind of a debutante, which is funny in a way because Tucker, N.C., is about as far as you can get from the social whirl and not fall into the Atlantic Ocean. Her dad is rich and owns, among other things, the store where Mama works, the only place around here you can buy groceries. All through school, Sue and I have been neck and neck gradewise. She loves to join organizations but I'd rather spend my time at one or two things I really enjoy, like playing volleyball in the fall, or working at the day-care center across the highway from the school. Maybe Sue and I get along because we're not out for the same things in life. Although we aren't bosom buddies, she's the closest female friend I have since Terri Turner moved to Norfolk last year.

I say "female" because, up until a couple of months ago, I had always thought of Jim as my real best friend. Since we were kids, he and I have gone fishing, worked in tobacco and on cars, gotten lost, and just generally hung out together. We could talk about anything—I mean *any-*thing. He and Grampa were always great pals, too. When Grampa died year before last, Jim cried as hard as I did.

But when Uncle Tate came to live with us last fall, he

made embarrassing remarks about Jim and me every chance he got. Nothing he said was true, but it seemed like just his saying it made both of us self-conscious. Jim gradually quit coming by. These days I only see him at school.

The room started filling up as soon as the first bell rang. Sue waved as she came in. "Missy! I was worried about you. The kids on Seventy-eight said you didn't ride this morning."

"I rode my bike," I said, going to my desk.

"All five *miles?* In this *weather?* God, Missy, what're you trying to do, get pneumonia? Why didn't you call me? I'd've picked you up."

She claimed her seat in front of me, bringing with her from the outdoors an invisible wrap of cold air.

"You wouldn't have wanted to be here that early," I said. "I had to see Ms. Hollins."

She pivoted in the seat. "Is something the matter? Have you got a problem?"

I'm always caught between wanting to laugh at Sue and wanting to shake her till her brain rattles. "No," I said, holding up my hand to ward off her care attack. If she'd been Terri, I would've told her everything, but Sue is not above bringing a person's deepest, darkest secrets into her everyday conversation. "It was just FAF stuff."

"I took the FAF home last night," she said. "Daddy says he's not even going to bother to fill it out. I don't qualify for financial aid—he makes too much money. Poor Daddy! He works *so* hard, but he'll have to pay every cent of my college education!"

I wondered, was she complaining or bragging? I tried

to work up some sympathy, but knowing what her dad pays Mama, I couldn't. "Maybe you should get a job this summer and help out," I said.

"Well, I *work* at the *store*," she said. "Daddy says he'd rather for me to do that than go to work for somebody else."

I thought of some of Mama's choicer comments about the way Sue "works," and stifled a snort. Luckily, second bell rang and Mr. Preston made us stop talking.

At lunchtime I took my apple and my peanut butter sandwich to the cafeteria, bought a carton of milk, and then threaded my way around tables and through noise looking for Jim. I found him at last in a far corner sitting beside Melanie Brown, deep in conversation. Their heads were almost touching. I turned to go to another table, but Jim had seen me. He beckoned with one lanky arm.

"Yo, Missy—c'mere and sit with us!"

"Looks like you're nearly through," I said. "I'll go—"

"We're not leaving yet," he interrupted, taking hold of my elbow. "Sit."

I did, throwing Melanie an apologetic look. She has had a crush on Jim ever since tenth grade, but she has a problem with me. How can a girl be a guy's friend but not a girlfriend, she wants to know? It'd probably help my case if I was dating somebody, but since I'm not, I mostly get on her nerves. When she's with Jim, I try to make myself scarce to prove to her my intentions are honorable.

Jim is a lean six feet five. His shoulders hunch slightly, probably because he's had to spend so much of his life bending over to listen to people who are shorter than he is. That, of course, includes me, although since I'm five-eleven he doesn't have to bend quite so far on my account as he does for Melanie, who is five-three.

"Are you doing day care this week?" Melanie asked, flipping her blonde curls back. It's a habit she has. One time in class I counted. She flipped fourteen times during the fifty minutes. But maybe I'm envious because mine is straight, plain brown, waist-length, and won't flip.

"Thursday and Friday afternoons," I said, unwrapping my flattened sandwich. "You?"

"I've signed up for Mondays and Tuesdays this month," she said. She smiled at Jim. "Those little kids are so cute. I could just squeeze 'em to pieces. I hope when I get married I have half a dozen."

"Whoa!" Jim laughed, leaning away from her. "You don't know what you're saying. I've got two brothers and three sisters, remember. It's too many, right, Missy?"

"I'm no expert, since I don't have any," I said, "but I've known Jim to sleep out under the stars in the bed of the pickup when things got too crowded inside."

Melanie pouted. Maybe she didn't like it that I knew more about the family than she did. "Three, then. I'd settle for three."

"It'll be a long time before I start worrying about things like *that*," I said, taking a large bite of sandwich.

"Yes. Jim tells me you're going to college."

The peculiar note in Melanie's voice made me quit chewing and look at her. Was she glad? Did she doubt it? Did she think the whole idea ridiculous? Was she jealous? I couldn't tell. "I hope so," I mumbled at last through peanut butter and bread.

"Well!" she said, pushing back from the table and giving

her hair another flip. "I have to go to my locker. You coming, Jim?"

"Nope. I'll stay here with Missy. I'll see you in English."

There was no mistaking from Melanie's expression what she thought of that, but if Jim caught on, he certainly didn't show it.

"You should've gone with her," I said, when she was out of earshot.

"Why?" he asked innocently.

I laughed. "Skip it." I slurped my milk through the straw, knowing it would make him laugh. We have always acted silly around each other.

"So what happened when you told your mom what you were going to do?" he asked.

"She was kind of stunned." I peered over the milk carton. "You know, I've been planning this for so long I guess I didn't calculate the effect it would have on her, hearing it for the first time. Trouble's ahead. Uncle Tate."

He nodded once, understanding. "Stay cool."

"Easier said than done." I slurped again. "He never listens."

Jim opened his mouth to say something, but the bell in the corner directly overhead clanged for the end of lunch period. I put my hands over my ears until it stopped. Jim was already getting up.

"English," he said, moving toward the door. "Ms. Pope says if I'm late one more time she'll take five points off my nine weeks' grade. I don't have five points to spare. See ya!"

I got to my feet slowly, munching on the apple as I

headed out of the cafeteria. Being college bound has put me on a different track than Jim, meaning we never have classes together anymore.

His life's ambition is to own his own fishing boat like his daddy and granddaddy before him. Although it gets harder and harder to make a living at fishing, what with the red tide and the fish kills from pollution, it's in his blood. Jim is smart, but he's never pushed himself to make more than just passing grades.

The truth is that, until ninth grade, I pictured myself as living here in Tucker forever. I didn't give much thought to how people made a living. Mama worked at the store. Grampa farmed and occasionally fished. I figured I would do something like that, too.

Then Ms. Hollins started saying things like, "Just keep up the good work and you'll get a college scholarship." Mr. Preston made me enter a project in the Science Fair every year. "It will look good on your college application," he'd say. When teachers encourage you like that, you start believing them. At least I did. For four years, I've had this dream in my head of myself in college, although I'll admit the details of the dream have been kind of fuzzy.

But since last night, the reality has begun to sink in and I'm beginning to wonder. It's kind of like planning to be a professional dancer and realizing all of a sudden that you haven't had any dancing lessons.

The bell rang for fifth period to begin and I had to break into a run to make it to Mrs. Arnot's class on time. She has a thing about people being ready to work as soon as the bell stops ringing. I tossed my apple core into the trash can and slid into my seat, psyching myself up to learn about History and Contemporary Issues. Mrs. Arnot is determined that the nine of us in this class will understand what we see on the television news and read in the papers. She wants us to be able to make intelligent judgments and not just believe what somebody tells us to believe. I often wonder how different Uncle Tate would have turned out if he could have taken a course like this when he was in high school.

Chapter 2

3:30 P.M. is the downside of the day this time of year. Add to that the clouds and mist lingering from last night's storm and you have bleakness in its rawest form. Not looking forward to the long ride with a north wind in my face, I unlocked the chain from around my bike wheel, put on my mittens, and pulled my old wool toboggan cap down low over my forehead and ears. Given a choice between being cute and being warm, I'll choose warm every time.

"Hey, Missy—wait a sec!"

I turned in the direction of the voice. Jim leaned out of the window of the Ranger, waving both hands.

"Come put your bike in the truck!" he hollered. "I'll take you home!"

My spirits lifted. I wheeled the bike toward the parking lot, but as I got closer, I saw another head inside the truck just beyond Jim's. Melanie's.

"Thanks just the same!" I yelled back, stopping in my tracks. "I need the exercise!"

I didn't give him time to say anything else, just turned the bike around, pushed off with one foot, and pedalled up the highway like I was being chased by wild dogs. No danger of him following. Melanie lives in another direction.

I went at top speed for over a mile before my leg muscles hollered and I sat back on the seat. My eyes watered, whether from the cold or other reasons I couldn't tell.

If I'd gotten into the truck with the two of them, I'd be the one sitting on the outside next to the door, and when they dropped me off and rode away, I'd be the subject of their conversation. Or I wouldn't. Either way, I hated it. And I hate January.

Pedalling slowly, I hugged the edge of the narrow highway, concentrating on keeping the wheel on the solid white line like a high-wire person performing at the State Fair. One wobble of the wheel and you're done for. The wide canal ditches on either side of the road brimmed with brown water. The gray mist beaded on my leather jacket. Even with mittens on, my fingers grew numb in the bitter wind.

I pedalled past Mr. Stark's pasture and Mrs. Slater's farm. Just beyond that is the little yellow house where Alma Dean Rodriguez lives and has her beauty shop. AY-DEE'S SHORT CUTS is burned into a wooden sign that swings on two hooks from a beam out front.

Mrs. Rodriguez is Mrs. Slater's daughter and originally from these parts, although as Gramma puts it, she ran off with a Cuban years ago. Since she's not the churchgoing type and I don't spent time in beauty shops, I haven't seen much of her since she came back alone to Tucker to live, but she's a regular customer at Gibbs's store. That's how Mama has gotten to know her and they have become friends. Mrs. R. is a large woman—Grampa would have called her fleshy—but not saggy. To judge by her fingernails, eyebrows, lashes, skin, and hair, it appears she practices her trade on herself. They're never the same color, shape, or style any two times I've seen her. If it weren't for her head-on personality, I might not recognize her every time.

Gramma has been down on her ever since Mama came home from work a couple of weeks ago with her dark hair cut short and curled close to her head. She looked like a magazine picture compared to before when she wore it shoulder length and bobby-pinned behind her ears.

Uncle Tate looked sour and quoted First Corinthians about a woman's hair being her glory. Gramma said she'd never trust Alma Dean Slater with *her* hair. "She'd as soon dye you purple as not," she declared. The way Gramma talks about Alma Dean, you'd think the woman was leading Mama down the road to sin and degradation.

Finally I could see the upper part of our house through the trees, glaring white even in this gray weather. It is one of the real old houses from before the Civil War, tall and wide with double chimneys at either side like flat bookends, and a screened-in breezeway streaming out the back like a fat tail. I rode the bike into the yard, thankful to be home at last. Then I saw Uncle Tate standing on the front porch wearing Grampa's old felt work hat, his legs braced apart like he'd been waiting for me. My heart sank as I remembered his announcement last night that he was being laid off of his construction job because of the bad weather. I had overlooked the fact that it would mean he'd be home all day.

"The bus came by an hour ago," he said as I approached. "Where you been?"

"I rode my bike this morning so I could get there early," I told him.

His eyes narrowed. "What's so important you've got to leave for school before any of the rest of us even get out of bed?"

"I had to see the guidance counselor." I wheeled the bike past the porch to the shed where we keep junk and dry firewood.

"You in trouble?" he persisted, going to the end of the porch so he could keep his eye on me, but not actually come out in the misty rain.

"No, Uncle Tate." I laughed, although I didn't feel like it. I *was* in trouble, and he was it, but it would be a cold day in July before I'd tell him so. "She's so busy this time of year, she doesn't have much time during the regular school day."

"Time for what?"

"To talk!" By this time, I was hollering from inside the shed, where I was locking the bike to a support beam. Out of his line of vision, I made a horrible face at him through the shed wall, but when I came out, I was as pleasant as could be.

14

Uncle Tate is not handsome, and by the looks of pictures in the family album, he never has been. Tall and gangly, with a skinny neck and shoulders just a shade too narrow, now that he's near fifty and has some middle-aged spread, he's more the shape of a yellow squash. It makes me wonder what sweet Aunt Mary ever saw in him.

"You better go on in there and help your Gramma fix supper," he said. He takes this head-of-the-family stuff seriously. He has certainly changed from the man he used to be. I can actually remember when I liked him, but the way he's acted since Aunt Mary died has wiped out the positive as far as I'm concerned.

I let myself in by the back screen door and scraped my wet feet carefully on the porch mat. Through the steamy kitchen windows, I could make out Gramma moving back and forth between stove and refrigerator. A spicy wave of baking gingerbread washed over me when I opened the door. Gramma looked up. Wisps of white hair straggled loose around her face and her glasses were fogged.

"Law, you like to scared me to death! I never looked for you to come in this way. Get on in and close the door before you let all the warm air out."

I obeyed, leaning against the door to make sure the latch clicked while I pulled off my mittens and blew on my reddened fingers. "Boy, it's cold out there!"

"It's supposed to be—it's January. Anybody'd ride a bicycle five miles on a day like this . . ."

She let it drop, but I got her meaning. I thought it interesting that she knew I'd ridden my bike but Uncle Tate didn't. She usually tells him everything.

"Do you need any help?" I asked, to change the subject.

"I sure could use some, if you can spare the time," Gramma was never one to hide her sarcastic streak, and it seems like she's gotten worse since Uncle Tate moved in.

"Give me three minutes," I said, already on my way toward the stairs, tugging at the damp jacket as I went.

Upstairs in my room I rushed about, hanging up the jacket, changing into dry shoes, making sure I'd brought home the books I needed to do my homework. I happened to glance in the mirror and saw that the cap had given me hat head, not to mention leaving vertical ridges across my forehead where the ribbing is so tight. I picked up my hairbrush and made a few halfhearted passes at my hair. I thought of Melanie's blonde curls.

Ah, well. A person can't just stand around moaning about things like that. I put down the hairbrush and was about to leave the room, when I noticed that my old straight brown curtains had been replaced by sheer, mint green ruffly ones. Gramma must've been working on them during the times I wasn't home. I had to admit they let in a lot more light on a rainy afternoon, but they made the rest of the room look like a grimy wall that's just had one spot accidentally cleaned. My gold-and-brown plaid bedspread didn't go too well with mint green ruffles.

I went downstairs slowly, thinking what to say to Gramma about the curtains. It's a tricky thing, thanking a person for something you never wanted in the first place. My old curtains were perfect for keeping out the first light of morning when I wanted to sleep. But Gramma's words

16

bite so sharply she has to find a way to show her other side. Making things for me is her way.

"Longest three minutes *I* ever lived through," she commented as soon as I came into the kitchen.

"I was looking at the curtains," I said. "They sure do brighten up the room. I appreciate the trouble you went to to make them."

"Glad you like them." She allowed her face to soften some. "Tate helped me hang them. We had to put up an extra rod for the crosspiece. You should thank him when you get the chance."

My stomach tightened. While my brain says it's perfectly reasonable for Uncle Tate to help Gramma fix things around the house, I don't like the idea of him being in my room, making judgments about my posters, my pictures, my magazines, or anything else about me.

"You hear me?" she said.

"Yes, ma'am." I opened the china cupboard and took down the plates.

When I heard the VW pull into the yard at last, I stopped what I was doing and went outside, with Gramma calling after me, "You better put on a jacket—you'll freeze out there!"

I felt like I had to have at least a minute with Mama before Uncle Tate and Gramma started in. She got out of the car, and when I hugged her, it seemed to me that I was hugging mostly coat. She is too thin and worried-looking these days.

"I couldn't believe you were already gone when I got up this morning," she said, as we walked slowly toward the house. "To tell the truth, it scared me. I wouldn't've been surprised if you'd been gone for good."

I was astounded. "Where would I go?"

"Away from here—I don't know." She stopped walking and looked at the house all lighted up, like she could see right through the walls into the living room where Uncle Tate watched Dan Rather, and into the kitchen where Gramma whizzed around among the appliances. She began talking fast, as though she feared she'd be interrupted and she had a lot to say.

"It's going to take a while for me to fill out all that stuff you brought home. I don't usually figure my taxes this early in the year. When've you got to send it?"

"Ms. Hollins says it would be best to have it in by February first. The colleges give out the money first come, first served."

Mama nodded, taking in the information. "Tate's dead against it."

"Mama, are you scared of him?"

She sighed. The puffs of vapor made her discouragement visible. "No, not scared of him. It's just that, these days, you can't reason with him. It wears a person down after a while."

"It seems like he's trying to take Grampa's place," I said. "He was even wearing Grampa's hat this afternoon."

"It'll take more than a hat," Mama said with scorn. "I wonder how he thinks we managed before he came?"

Actually, we three females did a pretty good job of pulling ourselves together after Grampa died. It wasn't easy, especially for Gramma and Mama, who tended to give in

18

to Grampa and let his word be law on most every subject. It didn't really matter whether he knew what he was talking about or not. He was the man.

But left to ourselves, we got more relaxed about things. For instance, we pared the evening meal down to one meat and two vegetables as opposed to the double portions of everything Gramma insisted on serving as long as Grampa was alive. Maybe if she hadn't been so conscientious about it, he would have lived longer, because he weighed too much and his heart gave out. But I personally would never say that to her because she was doing what women around her have been taught to do since time immemorial—feed their men.

Now that Uncle Tate's here, she has reverted to her old ways—two meats, four vegetables, two kinds of bread, and dessert. Every night. She claims she wouldn't want to do any less for him than Aunt Mary did.

The porch light came on suddenly and Gramma opened the door.

"Are y'all going to stand out there in the cold all night? Tate's ready to eat!"

Mama gave me a sidelong look that almost made me laugh. "We're coming," she said, leading the way up the steps.

Chapter 3

All through supper, I sensed a difference in Mama, something I couldn't quite put my finger on. Uncle Tate tried to get a rise out of her. Once he referred to her "shaved head," but she let it go by without comment. Finally he said, "Ruth, I spoke to Ma about this. I want you and her and Missy to consider changing your church membership over to Foursquare Gospel Fellowship."

I nearly blew mashed potatoes all over the table. I have been a member of Sandy Hill Missionary Baptist Church since I was baptized at age eleven, and I was on the Cradle Roll from the day I was born. Great-Grampa Field was a charter member of the congregation back in the 1800s.

Mama looked up from eating. "Why?" She was so calm, you would have thought he had suggested changing the bed linens.

"Because it's a sanctified church. Lamar preaches the true word of God, not to mention he was a great comfort during Mary's illness, unlike some others I could name."

He was referring to our pastor Mr. Webber, who is a youngish man not many years out of seminary. Soon after Aunt Mary died, Uncle Tate left Sandy Hill and started going to this other church.

"Well, that's fine for you," Mama said, "but I intend to stay at Sandy Hill."

"Me, too," I echoed. "I don't believe Grampa would want us to change over *without any good reason.*" I came down good and hard on the last four words.

Gramma was silent. I felt pretty sure that Uncle Tate's arguments had been raining about her head and shoulders the entire day. It's hard for anyone to bear up under such persistence, especially someone like Gramma who has such a blind spot where her son is concerned.

Of course he expected us to resist. He thrives on it, so our refusal didn't disappoint him.

"There has to be a better reason for belonging to a church than just because you've always gone there," he said sanctimoniously.

"Yes, and there has to be a better reason than just because somebody thinks you *ought* to, too," I said.

"Missy's right," Mama spoke up.

By this time, Uncle Tate had caught on that something *was* different about her and he went after it, determined to stomp it out before it multiplied.

"Hah! It's just that kind of thinking that ruined you in the first place!" he proclaimed. "And now you encourage it in your daughter, who's about to go and make the same mistakes *you* did!"

For just a fraction of a second Mama wavered, but then she came back at him. "It doesn't matter what you say, Tate. I'm not changing my church membership for you or anybody. Ma can if she wants to. So can Missy, if she wants to, although I expect hell to freeze over first."

"Ruth!" Gramma gasped, plainly shocked.

I was so proud of Mama my chest filled with fresh air and I almost hollered. But I didn't. Instead, I turned to Gramma and asked point-blank: "Are *you* going to change?"

The muscles of her face all pulled toward her mouth, which puckered in dozens of tight little lines like stitches around a buttonhole. "I'm thinking about it," was all she said, but it was enough for Uncle Tate to gloat and declare that at least one person in the family besides him had some sense.

When we finished the meal, I helped clear the table and wash the dishes before going up to my room. I used to do my homework at the dining-room table while Mama crocheted or read and Gramma pored over her Sunday-school lesson or knitted. Sometimes we watched TV. It was a peaceful, pleasant time.

Now Uncle Tate has taken over the TV to watch what *he* wants to watch. That wouldn't be so bad if he didn't keep up a running commentary of opinion throughout the program. I've finally given up trying to do any work downstairs.

Propped against a couple of pillows, I lay on top of the

plaid bedspread surrounded by books and papers. I stared at the opposite wall where my poster of Albert Einstein hung, but I wasn't really seeing it. The room's chill seeped through my wool sweater and socks. I thought about Jim and Melanie and felt again the surge of . . . what?

Jealousy.

I was the one who said it, but it was like another voice hissed the word, shocking me to sit straight up. I got off the bed and sort of walked around and around in the little space between the chest of drawers and the bed.

Why should I be jealous? Jim was my friend, the one person, now that Terri was gone, that I was willing to trust myself and my secrets with. Until this thing with Melanie, I didn't realize how much I had depended on his being there when I needed him.

So it was a kind of jealousy, although I hated the word. I stopped circling and sat on the edge of the bed.

The knock on my door startled me.

"Yes?" I hastily grabbed up a book and leaned back on the pillows, to look as though I was hard at work.

"It's me," Mama said.

I leaped up and opened the door wide. "Come on in," I said, giving her a hug before shutting the door. "You were so *good* telling Uncle Tate where to get off. I wanted to yell!"

"It's a good thing you didn't," she said. "No need to make things worse than they already are." She folded her arms across her chest. "Missy, it's *cold* up here. We have to get you a little heater. Maybe next time I get paid . . ."

"I wear lots of layers. Here—put on my bathrobe." I

handed her the aqua chenille robe I'd inherited from Aunt Mary. The sleeves come almost to my elbows and the hem isn't much below my knees, but I only wear it up here.

"I want to talk about this college business," she said, sitting on the bed beside me.

I got very still inside, afraid even to guess what she might be going to say.

"I should've known what you were planning," she began. "I guess you knew what you'd be up against, though, if you brought up the subject."

"Maybe I'm a coward," I said.

"Maybe you're just smart," she replied with a smile. "Seems to me you have your plans pretty well laid out."

"Mama, you haven't said what you think," I said.

"Haven't I?" She sat up a little straighter, making the bed bounce. "Well, I think you should go. I want you to."

I purely got a lump in my throat. I leaned forward and hugged her again. "*You* sure aren't a coward," I said.

She held me away from her and looked me in the eye. "About some things I am," she said. "But I'm trying to change that."

I thought of all she'd put up with from Grampa, Gramma, and now Uncle Tate. Eighteen years was a long time to have to pay for one mistake. If it was a mistake. I didn't know very much about the details. I'd never come right out and asked her to tell her side of the story.

"Mama," I said, "tell me about when you were at Carolina."

Her eyes shifted from mine to a point just over my right shoulder. "What do you want to know, exactly?"

"Just what happened." I tried to sound casual. "The fill-ins."

"All right!" she said with an energy that made me blink. "I'll tell you. It was about the time that rules for students were being relaxed in colleges all over the country. And here I'd come from a place where there was a rule for practically everything, even when to pee. I couldn't handle the freedom. I know it was dumb of me, but I was no older than you, and I had a lot less common sense."

She stopped for a moment, but she wasn't being careful like she often is when we talk, choosing just the right words, leaving out a lot. "Long as I was at home, Pa wouldn't let me date. He said I had to be at least eighteen, and of course I only turned eighteen in late summer, right before I left.

"At Carolina, it seemed like boys were coming out of the woodwork. Even a little nobody like me could go out every night if she wanted to. And I did. I'd been nothing but responsible ever since I could remember, and now I wanted to play."

"Was it fun?" I asked.

"It sure was! I was two hundred miles from anybody to shush and shame me. That was the best part of all. I studied, too, and made average grades—good enough to stay in school. But at the end of the year, when I came home for summer vacation, I nearly died."

"Why?" I asked. "What happened?"

"Nothing. That's just it. The only job I could get around here was handing tobacco. I didn't have anybody to talk to. Going to college had put a wedge between me and most of my high school classmates. I missed the campus, I missed my friends. It was like . . . it was like somebody lowered a two-ton concrete slab on me, and it was pressing down, pressing down."

I'd never heard Mama talk like that. She was like another person.

"Well," I said, "at least the second year, you didn't have to fight with Grampa and Gramma about going back to school."

"It was more a case of them not having an excuse to stop me," she said. "I was a student in good standing. When I left to go back to Carolina for my sophomore year, I'd already made up my mind I'd never spend another summer in Tucker."

"So then what happened?" Although it was a story with an ending I already knew, I wanted to know the path of it.

"It started out fine. I buckled down, determined to make all A's on midterms, or to come as close to it as possible. I'd only go out on weekends. And then—"

She stared into space, seeing scenes I couldn't see. I was almost afraid to swallow, for fear of disturbing the mood.

"—then I fell in love, or thought I did. No, I *did*." She corrected herself. "Just because he went off doesn't mean I didn't love him."

This was the person named William Harvey Cord, Bill, whose name was on my birth certificate.

"I met Bill at a rally. He was an activist, one of the people on campus who spoke out against the war and for civil rights. He wasn't afraid of anyone in authority, or so it seemed to me. I flipped. Everything he believed in became important to me. It was like the scales fell from my eyes. I saw that I'd lived blind to injustice for all of my nineteen years and that I needed to be about the business of changing things."

"I can see how that wouldn't sit too well with Grampa," I said.

"Well, at first he and Ma didn't know about it. But then there was a feature story in the *N & O* about student demonstrations and they saw me in one of the pictures."

I could imagine Grampa's rage and embarrassment, knowing he couldn't do a thing about what had happened.

"I came home for Christmas vacation," Mama went on. "I wouldn't have, but Bill was going out to Illinois to visit his family and I didn't have anyone to be with. Pa was awful. He'd go from not speaking to me, to yelling at me, to not speaking to me again. He called me names. In church he stood and asked the preacher to pray for my immortal soul."

"What about Gramma?" I asked.

"Now, Missy—you ought to know the answer to that," she said gently. "Besides, they were scared. They'd lost control of me."

I shook my head. "I don't know how you can be so calm about it. I think if I were you, I'd be furious right to this day."

She shrugged. "Well, I was still a kid. I talked big, but when I found out I was pregnant, I was terrified. I mean numb—panicked. My brain wouldn't work."

"You weren't married, then." I said it, but it was more a question.

"No." She shook her head, watching me. "We got married."

I tried not to think too much about that. "So when did he . . . go away?"

"At the end of the semester, he made plans to go to Illinois—to tell his folks about us, he said. In person. By that time, I was five months along. I thought he and I would stay in Chapel Hill. We'd both get jobs and I'd work as long as I could. I looked ahead to the fall. He'd keep going to school. I'd finish after he did, when the baby was a little older."

The baby. That was me, but she was talking about it as though it wasn't real. I guess back then it . . . I . . . wasn't very real.

"When did you know he wasn't coming back?"

"One part of me expected him back within two weeks," she said. "The other part knew when I told him goodbye that I was seeing him for the last time. He'd gotten so he wouldn't look me in the eye anymore. He was restless, always pacing. When I didn't hear from him after a week, I called the number in Chicago that he said was his parents'. It turned out to be the number of a department store."

I was dumbfounded. "But didn't you ever hear from him?"

She shook her head. "Never again."

"The stinker!" I got up off the bed and started pacing again. "The dirty dog!"

"I called him worse things than that," Mama said. "I tried tracing him, using the University's records, but he had covered his tracks very well. Most of the information they had about him was false, as it turned out. Maybe he'd done it that way because campus activists were under FBI scrutiny. I don't know, but he was gone for good."

"Lord!" I exclaimed. "I sure hope I didn't inherit any of *his* genes."

"You needn't get all fired up over Bill Cord, because he's not worth it," she said. "But a girl needs to know what she's up against. If anybody'd told me when I was your age that my life would turn out the way it did, I'd never have believed it. I thought I had plenty of sense. But a person's feelings can be a hundred times more powerful than her reason." She paused. "And I think that's especially true when a person falls in love."

I went back to the bed and sat down on the edge, digging my heels into the brown woven rug, trying to take in what I'd heard. Mama was quiet, waiting.

"How've you *stayed* here all these years?" I asked finally.

"I don't know," she said. "Up to last night, I could've given you a half-dozen perfectly good answers to that question, but now I know none of them would be the truth. The point is, I have stayed here, and this is where you've grown up, and now I wonder if it was the right thing to do."

Chapter 4

I stood at the edge of the highway, waiting for the bus. Frost lay white on the flat fields, like a dusting of snow. Everything crunched underfoot—the crusty mud, the dead leaves, the stubble of grass. My nose stung in the biting cold and I wished I had a ski mask instead of just my old hat-head cap. It seemed to me that I had been awake forever, thinking about Bill Cord deserting Mama with never another word. I thought about her giving up everything she'd hoped for in life because I showed up. I made up new endings for the story where she and I— meaning before I was born—do not come back to Tucker but go to live in some other state or country or maybe stay in Chapel Hill. I would be graduating from Chapel Hill High School this spring. I would be their top student, and on my way to Harvard or Yale. Or maybe I wouldn't.

But no matter how I tried to change the scene, it ended up right here. Except for an occasional car passing, everything was so still I could hear twigs of trees snapping in the cold. Way off in the distance, the grinding roar of Number 78 came closer and closer. In a little while, the orange bus appeared, looking brighter than it really was against the gray landscape. With a hiss of brakes the stop sign swung out and the doors opened with a squeaking flourish. Would Bill Cord laugh if he knew his daughter lived in Tucker, N.C., where the most exciting event of a winter morning was a stopping school bus?

Tawanda Midyette, the driver, flashed a smile as I stepped up into the bus. "Hey, Missy—where you been?" She put out a hand and I gave her five.

"I rode my bike yesterday," I said, plopping into the seat right behind hers. She makes the others leave that seat vacant for me. Since I'm the only senior riding the bus, she claims I help keep things under control.

Not that she needs me. Nobody gets out of hand on our bus. No one can stand up under the force of a tongue-lashing from Tawanda, but she is never mean. She just knows how to make a person feel ashamed.

"I tooted the horn till your uncle came out and waved me on," she said, getting the bus underway again. A car zoomed around and sped up the road. "I was afraid you overslept yourself."

"No," I said, leaning my head against the window. "I've got three people in my family to make sure that'll never happen."

Usually Tawanda and I carry on a shouting conversation

all the way to school, but this morning, I didn't have the energy. When we arrived, I waited until everyone got off before I stood up, even though as a senior, I have the privilege of getting off before anyone else.

"You sick, girl?" Tawanda's forehead wrinkled.

"No," I told her, trying to make light of things. "I got here so early yesterday, I'm just dragging my feet to make up for it today."

I smiled when I said it, but she gave me a stern look. "You riding the bus this afternoon?"

"I have to work," I said. "I'll see you tomorrow morning. I'm really okay—just sleepy."

"I hear you," she said with a sniff.

Inside the school, I made my way to the locker, more than ever aware of the jostling bodies and the noise. I thought of a stick floating in the Sound, whirling in eddies or pushed along by the current.

"There you are."

It was Jim, looking down at me as though I'd let the air out of his tires or hid his English notes. Although I had done neither, I felt guilty. I tried for innocence.

"What's up?" I asked.

"What's wrong with you?" he said. "You took off up the road yesterday like you were mad at me or something. All I did was offer you a ride."

I turned back to the locker and got a book I didn't really need. "Well, I was in kind of a weird mood. I thought the exercise might do me good."

He looked at me like he didn't believe a word of it, like he was waiting for me to tell the truth. And I almost did.

32

I was right on the edge of it, when Melanie turned up and fastened herself to his arm.

"Hi, Missy!" She smiled, but the smile was for Jim, not for me. "Gal, you must have some leg muscles! Have you ever thought about being on a bicycle racing team?"

My face burned. I was 99 percent sure she'd made that very same remark yesterday afternoon. Was she suggesting that I had legs like tree trunks? "No," I said. "I don't have enough experience pedalling uphill."

Jim looked from me to Melanie trying to figure us out, but being such an uncomplicated person himself, he didn't get it. It was just as well.

"I'll see you guys," I said, moving away into the stream of bodies.

I made it to homeroom just as the bell rang. Sue was already in her seat.

"This may be a historical first," she said, as I dropped my books on the desk. "I don't ever remember getting here before you. Where've you been?"

"Thinking about skipping school," I said, wondering where that answer came from.

Sue's eyes widened. The next words were predictable. "What's wrong?"

Already I regretted my rashness. "Just kidding." I forced a smile. I sat in the desk and looked around the room. Mr. Preston stood at the lectern checking the roll. He doesn't have to call our names because he has taught all of us math or biology since we came to Wyndham High.

"Is it a guy?" Sue whispered.

"Is what a guy? I don't know what you're talking about."

She didn't try to hide her exasperation. "The reason you're late!"

Her loud whisper was heard by everyone around us. Chuck Bishop, in the next row, grinned at our little drama. Behind him, Maria Watson cupped a hand around one ear and leaned toward us.

"I wasn't late," I mouthed.

Sue turned to face the front. She tore a sheet from her notebook and wrote. Shortly she handed me a folded note:

> *I'm having a party at my house Saturday*
> *night from six until. You can bring a date.*

She watched my face as I read. She knew I wouldn't have a date. What did she expect me to do, jump up and down and clap my hands? I'd rather be almost anywhere than home Saturday evening, but a party at Sue's didn't float my boat either. On the same piece of paper, I wrote:

> *Thanks. I'll let you know.*

I folded it and handed it back to her.

Mr. Preston asked about some of the students who were absent. He reminded us of final semester exams in two weeks, as if any of us could forget. He read from a list of deadlines for seniors—graduation invitation orders, money for cap and gown rental. My eyes closed. My mind drifted. I saw Mama sitting here in this very classroom twenty years ago. She was confident, full of dreams, not thinking of being married or pregnant but of being a student, earning a degree, getting a job. I felt sorry for her. I wished she'd never laid eyes on Bill Cord.

But then I wouldn't be here.

I opened my eyes quickly, glancing around to see whether anyone was looking. My scalp prickled. I had the weird feeling that if I hadn't opened my eyes, I would have vanished.

All day I was pursued by what I knew. In the day-care center that afternoon, Mama's words came back to me. *A person's feelings can be a hundred times more powerful than her brain . . . especially in love.*

I was right on the edge of crying, a rare thing for me. I thought back over the people I'd had crushes on. There have been guys in my class and in the classes ahead of ours that I worshipped from afar, along with a couple of teachers and the seminary student who worked at our church last summer. But as far as I knew, I'd managed to get through my entire high school career to this point without disturbing anyone's heart rate.

Although Mama was not strict with me about going out with boys, it didn't matter because none had asked me out. It occurred to me that I had the potential to be just as desperate as she was at my age, maybe more so. If anyone paid me any romantic attention, no matter how dishonorable their intentions, I doubted I'd have the will to resist.

Why couldn't I be more like Sue? Guys were as usual in her life as mealtimes. I knew she'd never be taken in by any fly-by-night male. She'd be on the lookout for somebody better than anything she'd seen so far, and it would take a lot of time and travel to locate such a person.

"Missy, would you check on Perry when you finish there, please?" Mrs. Tilley's voice called me back to reality. Lost in thought, I'd been putting jackets and hats on the day-care children without even realizing it.

"Yes, ma'am." I finished tying a small shoe and then went into the adjoining room where Perry had wandered. It was after five and parents had begun arriving to pick up their kids. Perry's mom was always the last one to get there. He sat by himself in one of the little chairs, sucking his thumb. His eyes had a distant look, as though he wasn't there. I could relate to that.

"Hey, Perry," I said, hunkering down beside him. "What're you doing in here all by yourself?"

He turned and gave me a smile around the busy thumb. Perry was small for a three-year-old, not even as tall as some of the toddlers, but where they were still chubby and bowlegged, he was like a tiny little man, well-coordinated and quick. We're supposed to treat all the kids the same, but Perry is my undeclared favorite.

"It's time to get your coat on—your mom'll be here in a little while," I told him.

Perry pulled his thumb out of his mouth with a juicy little pop. "Is it five-thirty?" he asked in his clear voice, like a grown-up.

"It's getting there."

He stood up with a sigh. Even when he is standing and I am squatting, he has to look up at me. I resisted the urge to sweep him up in my arms and squeeze him. He'd let me, but I already knew the expression I'd see on his face—

patient, tolerant, waiting for me to get over my fit. The thought of it made me laugh.

He looked startled. "What's funny?"

"I thought of a joke," I told him, and then felt guilty for not being truthful. I amended my statement.

"Actually, I was just thinking I'd love to hug you, but I bet you couldn't stand it."

Perry laughed. He threw his arms around my neck, taking in my hair and everything. He lifted his feet from the floor and swung free, tugging me down. Last of all he gave me a wet, smacky kiss on the cheek. Something out of joint inside me slipped back into place.

"There!" he said, letting go and stepping back. He grinned from ear to ear, totally satisfied with himself.

"That was great," I said. "It's the best hug I've had all day."

"How many did you have?" he asked, interested.

"Only one," I told him. "From my mama."

"That's not many," he commented, holding up one finger and looking at it like a judge. "You need this many." He spread out all the fingers of one small hand. Then he added the other hand. "Or this many."

"I guess I'll just have to depend on you, then," I told him as we headed back to the big room for his jacket and hat.

Chapter 5

Riding home with Mama in the early dark, drained of energy, I could still feel Perry's arms wrapped tightly around my neck.

"Are you sure you're all right?" Mama asked.

"Yes'm. Just tired."

"You aren't coming down with something, are you?"

"No, ma'am. And it's not time for my period, either," I said, to head off the question.

"I've been a little worried about telling you all that stuff last night," she said. "Maybe it was too much at once."

She sounded as if she hoped I'd deny it. I did take a deep breath to do just that, but what came out was, "Look, I asked you, didn't I? If I'm not mature enough to hear the truth, then that's my problem."

"That's not the point," she said. "I don't care how old

a person is—eighteen or forty-eight—hearing the unvarnished truth about your parents and your own origins is bound to be unsettling."

I certainly couldn't argue with her there. I slouched farther down in the seat, pressing my knees hard against the dashboard.

"I'd like to run by Alma Dean's before we go home," she said after a few minutes of silence. "Is that okay with you?"

Other than being hungry, I was in no rush to get home. Uncle Tate would be there waiting, primed to pick a fuss with one or both of us. "Sure. Tell her she did a super job on your hair."

"Come inside with me and tell her yourself."

"I don't think so," I said. "I feel out of place in beauty shops."

"You wouldn't in this one. Alma Dean Rodriguez is different."

"Did you know her before?" I asked.

"Sort of, but we weren't friends then. She graduated from high school when I was in seventh grade. That's a big age difference when you're young."

It's true. I can't see myself hanging out with any of the seventh graders *I* know. "Gramma says she ran off with a Cuban."

"You have to take what Ma says with a grain of salt, Missy. He was from somewhere in South America, actually, and 'running off' is an expression people around here use for marrying someone your parents don't approve of, regardless of the reason. It's true Alma Dean didn't get married here in Tucker, but she would have if her folks had been a little more understanding."

Mama slowed the car to make the left turn across the canal ditch into Mrs. Rodriguez's yard. In addition to the porch light, a spotlight fastened to the post above the swinging sign made the letters on it clearly visible even at night. Through the front window, I could see a person draped in a plastic bib under a dryer, and Mrs. Rodriguez with her sharp-nailed fingers wielding a comb over an anonymous head.

"Maybe I'll just wait out here for you," I said.

"Oh, come on," Mama coaxed. "I want you to see the shop."

I followed her across the yard and up the steps to the tiny porch lined with flower boxes in which nothing bloomed. We walked straight in without knocking. I suppose people who do business at home get used to that.

The beauty shop was an overheated one-room affair, already crowded with its two customers and Mrs. Rodriguez. I squinted under the bright fluorescent lights. The odor of oils, conditioners, shampoo, perming solution, and hair spray hung sweetly thick in the air.

"Oh, hi, Ruth!" Mrs. Rodriguez sang out. "Come on in. I was just telling Mom about that haircut I gave you. See, Mom?" She spoke to the person under the dryer. "Isn't that smart? Turn around, Ruth, so she can see the back."

Obediently, Mama did a couple of turns in the tiny space. Mrs. Slater's eyes, hooded by the dryer, were impossible to read. "It's nice," she said in a flat voice.

40

The oily-permed customer in the chair was more enthusiastic. "A-law, Alma Dean, why didn't you do *mine* that way?"

"It wouldn't work for you, Sheila," Mrs. Rodriguez said. "Ruth has natural curl." She looked past Mama at me hovering near the door. "Well, Missy, did you come for yours?"

"My what?"

"Your style. I thought maybe after you saw how good your mom looked, you'd want me to do you."

My face burned. Painfully aware of my stringing-down hair now that she'd called everyone's attention to it, I was rather short with my answer. "Not in a million years. Took me too long to grow it."

Tonight Mrs. Rodriguez's hair was a striking auburn that flared out from her head in bold curls the size of snuff cans. Orange false fingernails and green eye shadow turned my mind to thoughts of Halloween. I hoped Mama would never let this woman talk her into a makeover. I leaned against the doorjamb, wishing I'd stayed in the car.

"There!" said Mrs. Rodriguez, expressing her personal satisfaction at Sheila's new do. She handed her a mirror and turned the chair around so she could look at herself front and back. "How does that suit you?"

Sheila patted the curls with a self-conscious hand and tried not to admire herself too much while we were all watching. "That looks *real good*, Alma Dean. I'm so glad you opened this shop, I don't know what to do." She turned to Mama. "I drove over here from Milway when I found out Alma Dean was back."

41

Mrs. Rodriguez untied the bib from around her customer's plump neck and tactfully averted her gaze while Sheila dug into a purse and brought up some bills, folded them, and pressed them into Mrs. Rodriguez's hand. In a few minutes, Sheila departed, brushing by me in a cloud of perfumery. I took a deep gulp of fresh air before the door closed behind her.

"Take off your coats and stay while I comb out Mom," Mrs. Rodriguez invited.

"No, we have to go on home," Mama said. "I just wanted Missy to see your shop."

Mrs. R. smiled, as though she already knew I wasn't the type who cared about the insides of beauty shops. "Come on back anytime," she told me.

I mumbled something polite and, as Mama lingered to say good-bye, opened the door and let myself out into the night. The shop's heavy sweetness clung to me as though Mrs. Rodriguez had aimed one of her aerosols at me and scored a direct hit. When Mama finally came out, I was already in the car.

"Well," she said, smiling expectantly as she got in and fastened her seat belt. "What do you think?"

"I think we stink," I answered with an exaggerated sniff.

"I mean about Alma Dean?"

What did she expect me to say? "She seems nice," I said finally, reminding myself of Mrs. Slater commenting on Mama's haircut.

But Mama herself didn't seem to notice. She hummed a little tune under her breath as we drove along. I felt a stab of envy. *I* should be the one who was humming.

42

I needed someone who wouldn't laugh or pity me or talk about it to somebody behind my back. By the time we got home, I'd made up my mind. Melanie or not, I had to talk to Jim.

I waited until everyone was settled in the living room for the evening before dialling Jim's number. I rarely call him up because with all those people in his family, both the call*er* and the call*ee* are subject to a lot of unwelcome teasing.

"H'lo?"

"Janine?" I guessed, picking at random the name of one of Jim's sisters.

"Naw, this is Hal!" came the disgusted reply. Then directly in my ear: *"Janine!"*

"I don't want to speak to Janine!" I hollered into the phone.

"What?"

"I want to speak to *Jim*."

"Well, why didn't you say so? *Jim!* Telephone! Naw, it's *not* for you, Janine, some girl wants Jim. *I* don't know." The voice came back to the phone. " 's this Melanie?"

"No!" I said. Sometimes I'm really glad I'm an only child.

After what seemed a very long time, during which I was privy to the considerable noise of the Perkins household, Jim's hopeful voice answered the phone. I hated to disappoint him.

"Jim, it's me—Missy. Look—could we talk? I don't mean on the phone. I've . . . I . . . there's something I need to ask you about."

"Well, yeah. Sure, I guess."

It depressed me that he didn't sound more willing. Tucker is not known for its meeting places, being more open fields and woods than buildings. That's okay if what somebody wants is a place to make out, but that wasn't what I had in mind. I tried to sound businesslike. "This won't take long. Meet me at Gibbs's store in twenty minutes."

"Okay," he said, and hung up. I went upstairs to get my jacket, wondering if I should be doing this. I felt sneaky, somehow, but shook off the feeling. Now was no time to chicken out. When I came downstairs, I stopped at the living room door.

"I'm going to borrow the car for a while," I said to Mama. "I'm meeting Jim at the store."

"Fine." She nodded. If she had questions, she didn't ask them. Uncle Tate, though, made up for it.

"What's this all about?" he asked, sitting forward in his chair.

"I'm going to meet Jim Perkins at Gibbs's store," I repeated. To myself I added, *If it's any of your business, which it isn't.*

"Why can't he come here to the house, like any other self-respecting young man?"

"Uncle Tate, we're not exactly talking romance, here."

"That's what *you* say." He looked meaningfully at Mama. "Things get out of hand sometimes."

At that point, I could happily have thrown the car keys at him. Mama lowered the afghan she was crocheting to her lap. "Tate, get your mind out of the gutter," she said. "All you think about is sex!"

I knew I'd better get outside quick. I bolted out the door into the cold night and managed to hold in my shrieks of laughter until I was inside the airtight VW where no one could hear.

But once on the highway, I felt myself sinking again into a blue funk. I tried to remember the old days when Jim and I dropped in at each others' houses anytime and didn't have to have a reason to call each other up. Tonight it seemed as though I were going to meet a stranger.

By the time I arrived at Gibbs's store, Jim's truck was already parked outside. Through the plate-glass windows, I could see him in the well-lighted store with his John Deere hat on, talking to Mr. Gibbs. They laughed about something. Jim tilted his head back and drank Pepsi from a can. Mr. Gibbs turned away with a grin on his face and poked buttons on the cash register.

What did Jim tell him? I wondered. Are they talking about me? Did Jim say why he was here? I can't go in there!

With no trouble at all, I worked myself into a state and was on the verge of going straight home, when Jim suddenly strode to the swinging door and stuck his head out.

"How long you been here?" he hollered.

I rolled down the window. "Couple minutes."

He came out and planted both hands on the window ledge. "Whatcha want to talk about?"

I shivered. "Come get in the car."

"*You* come sit in the truck," he said. "I have to fold myself in three parts to get in that little bitty thing."

Reluctantly, I followed him over to the truck, less than ever sure of myself the farther I got from my own territory.

He climbed into the driver's seat and I went around to the other side and opened the door. The truck, as always, smelled faintly fishy, its floor littered with crabline and tools. At least dating Melanie hadn't made Jim clean up the junk. I rested my sneakers lightly on top of it as I have always done when riding shotgun.

"My curiosity's about to kill me," he said. "What's up?"

I had refused to think about what I'd say to him when the moment came. Now, when I opened my mouth, nothing came out but vapor puffs.

Jim shifted slightly in the seat, waiting as seconds of silence passed.

"Jim," I finally blurted. "What if Uncle Tate's prediction comes true?"

"What prediction?" Jim never paid a whole lot of attention to Uncle Tate's ranting, taking him to be three bricks shy of a load anyhow.

I told him some of the story Mama had told me, about how she had never been allowed to date before she turned eighteen, and how she had made up for it with a vengeance once she got to Carolina.

"Just because of what happened to Mama, he's convinced that, if I go off to college, I'm going to get mixed up with some guy and lose what little sense I've got, not to mention my virginity."

There! I'd said it.

To my astonishment, Jim threw back his head and hollered with laughter. My insides shrivelled into a raisin-sized knot.

"What's so funny?" I asked through clenched teeth.

46

"Missy, that won't happen to you. Not in a hundred years."

"Why do you say that?"

"Well, because." He chuckled again. "You're not the kind of girl that a guy would—what I mean is—" He began to trip over his own words, as though once he'd gotten into it, he began to see pitfalls that hadn't been obvious to start with. "What I'm saying is, guys won't be chasing you around or anything," he finished. "I mean, you don't encourage it."

"But I *might*," I persisted, "if somebody *did*. How do I know?"

Jim studied me thoughtfully. I could see his face in the light from the store. "Now let me get this straight, Missy. Are you scared your uncle's prediction *will* come true or *won't* come true?"

I gasped. "Jim Perkins, what're you talking about?"

"Well, it sounds to me like you halfway wish he was right."

"That's not so!" I yelled, much too loud for the small space we were in.

Jim threw up both hands in front of him and ducked like he used to do when we were kids and he'd tease me beyond the breaking point.

"I thought I could talk to you about this because we've always been friends!" I shouted, reaching for the door handle. "I didn't think you'd make fun of me. I guess I know better now, don't I? Just forget I said anything. I'd really appreciate it if you wouldn't mention this to Melanie! But I guess that's too much to ask!"

I yanked on the door handle, but Jim grabbed my arm before I could get out.

"Now, just hold on," he said, raising his voice to match mine. "I'm not making fun of you."

"Oh, no? What about all the laughing?"

"I'm sorry I laughed. I thought you meant it as a joke."

"Some things just aren't funny," I muttered, but I didn't get out. I looked through the window on the passenger side so he wouldn't see my eyes watering. I knew well enough why I'd yelled at him.

"Missy," he said quietly when I didn't speak, "what do you want me to say?"

I sighed. "*I* don't know, Jim. Maybe I want you to tell me what I need to do."

"About what?"

"You're a guy," I said.

"So I've been told."

"Quit trying to be cute! This is serious."

"Okay." He settled with his back against the door, waiting again.

"I'm a normal female like anybody else," I said. "I'd like to be asked out once in a while, so . . . so it wouldn't be a big deal. I mean, that was Mama's downfall. Having boys ask her out was a big deal."

I could tell from the expression on Jim's face that he'd begun to wonder whether I'd lost my marbles.

"So," I stumbled on, "why *don't* any guys ask me out? What do I need to do so they will?"

Time crept by. Jim cleared his throat, shifted his leg on the seat, pulled at his hat visor. "Well," he said at last, "I always thought you were kind of . . . you know . . . satisfied with yourself the way you are."

"I *am*. I mean, I *have* been." It was so hard to explain. "Just answer my question, will you?"

"It's hard," he said. "You and me've been kind of buddies. I never thought about you as a girl."

It was the hardest blow of all. "Not ever?" I asked.

"I don't think so," he replied carefully, leaving a tiny bit of room for doubt or hope, depending on a person's point of view.

"Well, try it," I said. "Think of me as a girl."

I wasn't the only one embarrassed now. Jim pulled the visor all the way down over his face, making gusty sighing noises the way a person does when they want to get out of something.

"I *can't!*" he burst out, pulling the cap off his head and turning around to face the windshield. "Why don't you talk to some girl about this, anyhow?"

Why, indeed! What girl? Sue? Melanie? Glaring at him, I pressed my back against the door and breathed out vapor like dragon smoke. I felt betrayed. What a chicken he was, after all!

Suddenly the store lights dimmed, a sign Mr. Gibbs was closing up.

"I have to go home," I said sourly, opening the door and sliding off the seat. "Thanks for coming."

"I thought you were going to say thanks for nothing," Jim said. To his credit, he looked unhappy. My heart softened some.

"Sorry I put you on the spot," I said. "Just forget we

49

ever talked. And please do me a favor—keep it to your-self."

"All right," he said. Then he added with just a suspi-cion of a smile, "Want me to cross my heart and hope to die?"

I slammed the truck door.

Chapter 6

Next day, I lost no time in accepting Sue's party invitation. I could tell she was surprised, but only for the blink of an eye. Then she squealed, hugged me, and said she was glad, and so forth. Her enthusiasm was hard to stomach, but I was in a grim and determined mood. I'd show Jim Perkins!

Saturday night, I dressed in my gray skirt and red sweater Mama gave me for Christmas. For a few minutes, I wrestled with my hair, discouraged by its lack of shape and character, by the way it dripped over my shoulders and down my back like a threadbare curtain. I tried a twist, a ponytail, a single braid, and a bun. In the end, I just brushed it and let it hang, which is what it seemed to have in mind to do anyhow. All the while I studied myself in the mirror, trying to be both objective and merciful.

I don't think I'm an ugly person. All my features are in the right place, my nose is straight, I have a square chin and clear eyes. That's the good news. The not-so-good is that I lack color, what with hair halfway between blonde and brown, eyes between green and amber, skin that won't really tan without creating freckles. Nothing about me seems certain.

I had hoped to get out of the house without bumping into Uncle Tate, but that was not to be. He stood in the kitchen looking out the window into the night. Or at least he pretended that's what he was doing.

"Where are you off to?" he wanted to know.

"Sue's," I answered shortly, opening the door.

"Not to study, I bet."

"No. To party." I gave him a straight look. He nodded, to let me know I'd confirmed his worst suspicions. I told him good night and went out, feeling his pious, condemning eyes on my back.

Although he'd been bossy all his life, Uncle Tate wasn't this kind of religious nag when Aunt Mary was alive. He loved her a lot. When she died of cancer, he somehow got the notion that her death was a punishment from God against him for not being religious enough, which I think is kind of a conceited way to look at things. That's why he has gone over to Foursquare Gospel Fellowship, a church of don'ts, and has forsworn all pleasures. Personally, I think it's kind of like closing the barn door after the horse has gotten out—nothing he does will bring poor Aunt Mary back.

The Gibbses don't live right on the highway like most

of the rest of us do. They built their new house four years
ago way back up in the woods, so you have to drive down
a winding, narrow dirt lane to get there. I don't understand
it. Folks around here fought for years to get paved roads
just so they wouldn't have to worry anymore about getting
mired down in mud or shaken to pieces by ruts. As far as
they're concerned, living off in the woods is not progress.
But I guess when you're rich you have to do things to
distinguish yourself from the common person, even if it
means reverting to the old ways to do it.

And the Gibbses are rich, no doubt about it. They have
one of everything, two of most, even a swimming pool,
which is unheard of in these parts where there's already
so much free water to swim in, fresh and salt. In addition
to the store, Mr. Gibbs owns farmland and beach property.

I drove along the bumpy little road, going extra slow
in case I should meet another car coming my way. After
a few minutes, I emerged into the huge clearing that used
to be somebody's cornfield. It was ablaze with light, like
a night football field, and in the middle of it stood the
Gibbs's two-story gingerbread fake-Victorian mansion.
Cars were parked all over everywhere, and even with the
VW windows closed, I could hear music, the bass throb-
bing like a boat engine in the Sound. Somehow I hadn't
expected a crowd.

Did I really want to do this?

I turned off the ignition and sat there for a while in the
lit-up night, trying to psych myself. I pictured myself walking across the lawn, opening the door, walking inside.
Looking cool.

I shivered. Cold maybe—not cool.

"Well, Missy," I said aloud, "if you don't like it, you can always leave."

But I'm going to like it, I assured myself as I trekked across the frost-covered lawn. It was part of my plan to like it.

In spite of the cold, lots of people were outside the house. Smoke rose in the air as those I recognized and some I didn't huddled in groups and puffed away. Nobody paid me any attention as I headed for the front door and rang the bell.

"Aw, go on in!" a male voice hollered. "Nobody can hear the bell."

I opened the great carved door and stepped inside. The unmuffled blast of rock music almost threw me back out. The live band set up in the huge living room was better suited for a stadium. I scanned the faces of people closest to the door and recognized no one.

Maybe I'd come on the wrong night.

"Missy! You did come!" Sue rushed in from another room, looking like a tropical bird in a deep green sweater dress and gold jewelry. She grabbed my arm, took my coat, handed it to someone, and steered me through the standing-around guests. The music throbbed and squealed, filling up the room and cutting off all possibility of normal conversation.

"There's somebody here I want you to meet," Sue yelled close to my ear. "He's real cute."

My heart turned timid within me. I pulled against her tugging hands, following my natural instinct to run. "Whoa—wait a minute!"

54

"Now, cut that out, Missy!" Sue was stern. "You're here and you're going to have a good time."

It's what I had come for, wasn't it? I'd get used to it.

"Why are all those people outside?" I shouted, as we made our way among the clumps of schoolmates and strangers. "Not that it's not just as well, since I don't think there's room for anybody else in here."

Sue laughed as though I'd made some clever joke. "Mom and Daddy would kill if they came home and smelled smoke—of *any* kind!" She poked my ribs with an elbow, to make sure I'd get her meaning.

"Your folks aren't here?"

"Are you kidding? Missy—do I look crazy? Don't answer that. They've gone to Richmond for the weekend."

"Oh." I turned that over in my mind. "They know about the party, though?"

"What are you—a private eye or something?" She flashed another smile. "Let me put it this way—they know I'm having a little gathering."

I took a fresh look around. If this was a little gathering, I didn't want to see what she would call large.

"You want something to eat or drink?" We were passing the bar at that point, where, I was relieved to see, the drinks were mostly of the nonalcoholic variety. Bowls of chips and dips, peanuts, and other edibles sat around on tabletops and shelves.

"Maybe later," I said. I didn't want to meet the new person with food stuck between my two front teeth.

By this time, we'd gotten as far as the family room, which is about as big as two of our living room. I thought about Mr. and Mrs. Gibbs and Sue rattling around in all this space. At least, though, we had moved far enough away from the band to talk without our neck tendons standing out.

"Wait a minute, Sue," I said. "Can't you kind of get me ready for this?"

"His name is Van," she told me, not slowing down a lick. "I'm not telling you anything else—it would take away the fun of finding out for yourself."

In the far corner of the room, in a furniture group of two sofas and two chairs facing, sat a bunch of guys and girls laughing and enjoying themselves. I saw right away that there was one more male than female.

"Y'all," Sue interrupted, making our presence known, "I want you to meet one of my friends and classmates, Missy Cord." She began telling me their names: Steve, Ted, Kevin, J. B.—who was a girl—Tina, Shelly, Tim, and last of all, Van.

I don't know what I had expected, exactly, but I experienced a twinge of disappointment at Van's ordinary looks. If I turned away, I'd be hard put to remember what he looked like. It occurred to me at exactly the same moment that he might be having identical thoughts about me.

"These are all my friends from Camp Sea Lover," Sue was saying. "They're spending the night here."

Sue is the only person from these parts who has ever been to Camp Sea Lover, which is for rich kids. Actually, folks from Tucker kind of laugh at the Gibbses for spending so much money to send her to a camp where people sail boats and swim and fish when she could do it for free right where she lives.

Van and Tina made room for me on the sofa between them. I studied them all as the conversation went on around me. Steve, a first-class show-off, liked acting and music. Tim and Kevin were jocks, Ted a politician, and Van—well, it was hard to tell. He didn't have much to say. The girls were, like Sue, highly made-up and stylish, like city people. They seemed to be acting a part, maybe one called Party Girl.

Sue left us to go play hostess, taking Tim with her. I felt like a kid in a department store who's lost her mama. I found myself smiling a lot without feeling like it.

"Hey! Let's dance!" Tina shouted suddenly. She pulled Kevin to his feet and the two of them began performing what, to me, were miraculous gyrations. Steve and J. B. joined them. I figured Shelly and Ted would be next, leaving Van and me either to do the same or look like log bumps.

"I think I'll go get something to eat," I said to no one in particular, standing up to show I meant business.

"Me, too!" Van leaped to his feet as though he'd just been waiting for an excuse. Right away I noticed that he was two inches shorter than me. I hunched a little, to sort of minimize the difference. We more or less moved together toward the food and drink, but I wasn't sure whether he was with me or just travelling at the same time.

We got some food and found a reasonably quiet place out of the main line of traffic. In about ten minutes, I found out he was from Raleigh, that he was going to Duke in the fall, that he was a computer nut and a drummer in a band. He found out that I didn't know yet where I was going to college, and that I liked little kids and fishing. After that, conversation came to a dead stop. When he started looking restlessly past my right shoulder, I excused myself to look for Sue and say good-bye.

I never found her, but I did find my coat on a bed in a back room. I got it and left. The smokers still held forth under the tree, although they may not have been the same ones.

The scene faded to a small bright spot in my rearview mirror, and then disappeared altogether, when the road curved.

Chapter 7

Mama and I got up before anyone else Monday morning. She came to my room and handed me the Financial Aid Form.

"There," she said. "It's done. Get Ms. Hollins to go over it before you mail it, to make sure we haven't left out anything. If they base the awards on need, you ought to get a million dollars."

We smiled at each other. She went on downstairs to start breakfast and I looked at the form and the income tax papers. If we didn't live with Gramma, I don't know how we'd make it. And since Gramma herself has no income but Grampa's social security, I guess she depends on Mama, too. I could see where Uncle Tate's moving in would be an economic plus, but it's a shame that people who don't get along have to live together because they can't afford not to.

I went to my dresser and got my savings passbook out of the top drawer. Since I started working at the day-care center, I've saved $1200. It seemed like a lot until I found out how much one year of college costs. Even in a state school, my twelve hundred isn't enough for half of half a year. If I go to Moriah, which is private, the total cost will be more than Mama's whole year's pay.

Just thinking about it made me sick to my stomach. I shoved the passbook back into the drawer.

Tawanda got us to school a whole ten minutes before the bell rang. I went directly to Ms. Hollins's office.

"Hello, Missy," Ms. Hollins said, standing aside for one student to leave and another to enter. "Everything okay?"

"Yes, ma'am. Sure is." I put the FAF in the In basket and made a thumbs-up sign. She smiled and nodded.

"That's great news! From here on, it's downhill."

I went to class with her words echoing in my ears. Although I know how she meant them, a person could interpret them either of two ways: from here on I'd coast, or from here on things would go from bad to worse.

Sue and I converged outside Mr. Preston's door. "What happened to you the other night?" she said. "When I saw Van wandering around by himself, I didn't know what to think. One minute you were there, and the next you'd disappeared."

"Your voice is too loud," I said, barely opening my mouth, to demonstrate how I thought she should be talking. We got interested looks as we made our way to our desks. "I *did* look for you, but couldn't find you." I gave her what I hoped was a meaningful look. "I figured you were occupied."

Sue giggled. "Well, maybe I was at that." Then she added: "Frankly, I thought you and Van would hit it off. He's such a nice guy."

A person can't really get mad at Sue because she has good intentions. There's no malice in her plots, but then there's not much thought, either.

"Yes, he's nice," I agreed, and then seeing the hopeful glint in her eyes I hastened to add, "but we didn't have a whole lot in common." I decided not to use the word "boring" unless driven to it.

The bell rang then and we had to stop talking. I was concentrating hard on a problem Mr. Preston had given us, trying to figure the next step, when Sue suddenly reached her right hand around backward beside the desk and waved a folded piece of paper at me. I took it and spread it out on top of my open Trig book.

> *If you don't already have a date for the JanDance, I know a real cute boy from Elizabeth City you can ask.*

On the bottom of the piece of paper I scribbled *You don't ever give up, do you?* But I didn't say no.

The JanDance is a Wyndham High tradition. After semester exams are over, everybody busts loose. The whole school is invited, from ninth graders right on up, and a person never has to worry about whether or not they have a date. In some ways, it's better than the Junior-Senior, because you don't have to spend money on flowers or expensive clothes and nobody is left out. The student council decorates the gym and people who have tapes or albums contribute them for the music.

To show you how socially backward I must be, I've gone every year since ninth grade and never thought twice about the fact that I didn't have a date. Although we're allowed to invite someone from another school, they have to be screened. That's ever since the time a girl brought a guy who was older than some of the teachers and he wore a black unbuttoned shirt and black pants and went around all slitty-eyed. I don't think he actually did anything wrong, but it made the faculty so nervous they made some nonloophole rules. Now you have to practically give the life history of the person if they don't go to Wyndham. Personally, I never thought it was worth the hassle, unless you were so much in love with somebody you couldn't enjoy the evening without them.

Now here was Sue suggesting that I invite a person I didn't know. And what if he was as boring as Van? Or what if he was stuck-up, or turned out to be some kind of a hood?

When the bell rang for the end of class, Sue swivelled in her seat and said, "Well?"

"I don't know," I said. "Let me think about."

"You always have to think about it," she fretted. We elbowed our way down the hall through the clots of people standing around or moving against us. "I mean, you don't have to be engaged to a person to go out with them, Missy."

She was right, of course, and I knew it. "I really will

think about it," I told her, as I stopped at the door to English class. "I'll let you know—but don't nag me."

She disappeared into the crowd, shaking her head as a person will when they've done everything in their power to help the downtrodden and the offer has been refused.

Later that morning, on my way to Physics, I felt a heavy hand clamp my left shoulder from behind.

"Don't be in such a hurry," Jim said in my ear.

"I've got two minutes to get to class," I said, but I slowed down.

"We've got to talk."

"What about?"

"*You* know." He gave me an exasperated look. "From the other night."

"I thought we'd finished that conversation," I said shortly.

"Maybe we did, but I've been thinking about it some more."

I stopped then. The hall traffic flowed around us on either side. "All right. When and where?"

"Don't ride the bus this afternoon. Come to the truck and I'll take you home."

"Okay." I allowed myself a smile. "See you after school, then."

The bell rang and I barely made it to the lab before the sound died away. But it was hard to concentrate on physics for wondering what Jim had in mind. Don't hope, I kept telling myself, not even sure what I meant. But I appreciated the fact that he hadn't written me off as crazy. Or, if he had suspicions in that direction, was at least giving me the benefit of the doubt.

When the last bell rang, I made a beeline for bus 78. I told Tawanda I had a ride and would see her in the morning.

"You check it out with Mr. Farnum before I leave," she said sternly. Tawanda takes personal responsibility for everybody who rides on her bus.

"Okay. I'll wave at you to let you know," I said.

Mr. Farnum, the teacher on duty, nodded when I told him Jim was taking me home. One advantage of being the school goody-goody is that teachers never question your motives.

With a light heart, I strolled over to Jim's truck. He wasn't there yet, but I opened the door and climbed in. Despite the outside chill, the cab was warm after sitting in the sun all day. I slipped the backpack off my shoulders and put it on the floor between my feet. The peculiar combination of fish and metal smells and some creosote mixed in brought up instant memories of all the times the two of us had ridden in this very truck before and after an all-day fishing trip.

Five minutes passed, then ten. All the buses left. Only a few students hung around the entrance to the school. I twisted about in the seat, looking through each window in turn to see if Jim was coming yet.

At four o'clock, he hurried across the schoolground toward the parking lot. To understate the case, waiting all that time had not put me in the best of moods. When he got near enough to see me, he smiled and hung his head.

I didn't smile back. I rolled down the window.

"I'm sorry, Missy," he began. "Ms. Pope made me stay in because I didn't hand in a paper that was due today. She made me sit there and write it under her nose."

If he expected sympathy from me, he wouldn't get it. "Why didn't you tell her someone was waiting for you?"

"I did! She said too bad for them." He threw the books into the back of the truck and opened the door to get in. That's when we both heard a familiar voice.

"Jim? Jim, wait!"

Through the rear window, I saw Melanie trotting in our direction, waving both arms in the air. I knew she didn't see me. I dreaded the moment when she would.

"Oh, shit!" Jim said with a great sigh. "Why didn't she go on home?"

Why, indeed? I thought with a sigh of my own.

"Oh," she said when she caught sight of me in the truck. Then nobody said anything for several seconds. Jim was the logical person to explain, since he'd had the idea. But he appeared to have been struck dumb.

"Well!" Melanie's voice would have chilled grapes. "I didn't know you already *had* a passenger."

I could have made it easier on him. I could have said, *You don't understand, Melanie. It's not what you think.*

But how did I know what she thought? For months, I'd been helping their romance by making myself scarce and she still didn't believe in my good intentions. So I just kept my mouth shut.

With considerable stuttering and pulling at his cap, Jim managed to communicate to Melanie that he'd made plans to take me home this afternoon, that he'd had to stay in unexpectedly, and that he'd had no idea she was still at school at this hour.

"You didn't tell me any of this at lunch," she said.

"Well, I . . ." He didn't finish. Maybe he had sense enough to know that a lot of excuses when you've gotten caught don't serve any good purpose.

In the late afternoon sky, the winter sun shining through the bare trees at the edge of the empty schoolground made them appear darker than usual. I fastened my gaze on them. I pretended I was invisible. At that point, I didn't really care what Jim and Melanie did. Mostly, I wanted to go home.

"I guess you don't have any other way to get home," Jim said to Melanie.

"No," she answered.

"Well, then, get in." He opened the door on my side and I moved over to make room for her. She wouldn't look at me.

We turned south out of the parking lot onto the highway, which meant he was taking Melanie first. The truck tires whined on the pavement, making rubbery bounces over the tarred cracks. Jim switched on the radio and strains of country music swirled around our ears.

I thought I was the only one you loved, the voice mourned, *but now I know you're seeing someone new.*

Yuck! My hands twitched in my lap, wanting to cover my ears.

Jim turned into Melanie's driveway as I'm sure he's done many times. The muscles of his jaw worked like something was alive under his skin. Maybe it was the words he was holding back, knowing they'd do more harm than good.

"Well, here we are," he said, braking, but not turning off the engine.

Melanie opened the door and climbed down, looking at him all the time with those large eyes.

"I'll call you," he said.

That must have been what she was waiting to hear, because she slammed the door then and walked toward the house without looking back.

Jim sighed again and turned the truck around in the gravel loop. As we headed back up the highway, he turned off the music.

"I guess I really messed up," he said. I noted the question in the sentence, and I recognized the tone. He wanted me to say he hadn't messed up.

"I guess you did," I agreed, looking out the window on my side.

"I should've told her we were gonna do this."

Well, I was of two minds about that. If he belonged to her, he should have. If he still belonged to himself, then what he did was his own business. I thought about having to let somebody know exactly what I was going to do every minute. Or having to know that much about somebody. It made me tired. Still, he would have saved himself an awful lot of trouble if he'd said to Melanie at lunch, *This afternoon I'm taking Missy home so we can talk.*

Of course I knew perfectly well why he hadn't. For one thing he couldn't stand the look she'd give him. For another, she'd ask a lot of questions, such as, what've you got to talk about? Why can't you talk to her here at school? Jim's honesty when you catch him head-on gives him two choices—he can tell the truth or keep his mouth shut.

"How about if we go to the dock?" he said, when he saw that I wasn't going to smooth over the wreck of the afternoon.

As we rode along, I looked at the sloping sun and wondered if Jim would think, at day's end, that I was worth the trouble I'd caused him.

Cedar Bay is where Jim's dad and the other fishermen around here keep their boats. This afternoon it was a mass of wavelets. The boats moored at the dock rose and fell slightly, as though the water under them was breathing. Beyond the mouth of the bay, the Sound stretched blue until it disappeared into a haze at the horizon. Jim and I have spent weeks of our lives here. The few people there ignored us as we walked out on one of the splintery piers all the way to the end. The steady wind blew cold.

"You warm enough?" he asked.

"Yes," I said. I shivered and dug my hands deep into my jacket pockets. Even with the toboggan cap on, my hair whipped and tangled about my face.

At the end of the pier, we leaned on the waist-high railing and looked out at the expanse of sky and water. It kept us from having to look at each other.

"I guess I'm dumb," he began. "It took me a while to catch on to what you were asking me the other night."

Instantly I was all ears.

"I finally saw what you meant," he went on. "Like, how for your mama the regular dating stuff wasn't allowed, so when she got out on her own she was like an alcoholic turned loose in a liquor store."

"Well, now, I wouldn't go *that* far!" I protested.

"Whatever." He waved his hand to keep me from interrupting. "You're worried you might turn out the same way because you think you're missing the same thing she was. Right?"

"More or less." It sounded bald, even silly, when he said it.

"So . . . you asked me why guys don't ask you out. Or what you need to do so they will."

He has a good memory, I'll say that much for him. I nodded, not so sure that I wanted to hear what would come next.

"It seems like you took it as an insult when I said I thought you were satisfied with yourself. I didn't mean it as an insult. The main thing I like about you is how you seem glad to be the way you are."

Now he flung both hands out to the wind in a kind of helpless gesture. "A person's not always having to *guess* about you."

"No mystique, huh?"

"What?"

"Nothing mysterious about me. Nothing to wonder about."

"Well, maybe I would've said that up till Friday." He shook his head. "Now I don't know."

Somehow of all the things he'd said, that last cheered me most. "Are you going to answer those two questions for me, Jim? I mean, honestly?"

He looked pained. "You aren't like other girls." He saw my face fall and hurried on. "I mean you're . . . you're—" He groped for a word and then gave up. "Okay—think about a piece of land."

The words seemed so totally off the subject I could only gape.

"Left like it is, it's one of a few. Develop it to where people come buy lots and build copycat houses, and what've you got?"

Did he expect me to answer that question? I kept my mouth shut.

"You don't appreciate that, I can tell," he said. "I guess I know how you feel."

"You can't possibly," I said with bitterness. I was shivering hard now, only partly from the cold.

Jim moved and put one arm around me. I stiffened, although a year ago, I would have thought nothing of it.

"I guess you could change the way you look." He sounded doubtful. "That's all outside stuff, though. It's the inside you that's awesome to guys. You're smart. You're good at a lot of things, even those that we're supposed to be better at. And I personally don't think you ought to hide the fact, just so somebody'll ask you out."

Neither of us spoke for a while. The sun moved down, down toward the treetops. The wind picked up as it usually does right about sunset, slapping water against the dock pilings, little waves rushing in.

"Thanks, Jim," I said finally, straightening to my full height. I smiled at him for the first time that afternoon.

"I do have sense enough to know when somebody's paying me a compliment."

We started walking along the pier toward the shore. I thought how neat it was to have a friend who didn't want to change me, even though I wanted to change myself. By the time we got back to the truck, I'd decided what I was going to do.

"Would you drop me off at AyDee's Short Cuts?" I asked.

"Well, sure. But it's getting dark. How'll you get home?"

"I'll call Mama from there," I said.

We rode along in comfortable silence. It was like old times in some ways, but I guess we both knew how temporary *that* was. He still had to deal with Melanie, and I—

Well.

Chapter 8

I crossed the brown stubbled yard to AyDee's Short Cuts, climbed the three steps to the porch, opened the door, and walked straight into the shop with its overpowering perfumery. I felt big-boned and out of scale, a giraffe visiting a rabbit hole.

Mrs. Rodriguez, in a rose polyester smock, was releasing Mrs. Burgess's hair from the curlers that had crimped it into little cylinders all over her head. The sharp-nailed hands moved, rapid and sure, as though they might be able to do the job even if they weren't attached to her arms.

I tugged at the toboggan cap and pulled it off. My scalp itched from hair turned the wrong way at the roots. "Mrs. Rodriguez," I said, "I need a haircut."

In a matter of seconds her eyes took me in, sized me

up, made notes, and came up with a plan. I could see it happen, like watching a program come up on a computer.

"Alma Dean," she said.

"Alma Dean," I echoed uneasily.

"Have a seat." She nodded toward the chair that sat under the dryer. "I'll be through with Mrs. Burgess in just a little while."

I obeyed, leaning forward a little in the chair to keep the dryer hood from bumping the back of my head. To-night Mrs. Rodriguez—Alma Dean—was a brunette with a French twist and blue eye shadow. She and Mrs. Burgess took up the conversation they'd been having when I arrived. I stole a glance at my watch. Nobody in my family knew where I was.

I watched, fascinated in spite of myself, as Alma Dean's swift comb turned the silver cylinders into a fluff all over Mrs. Burgess's head. Mrs. Burgess smiled at her reflection the whole time. Clearly, she liked the way she looked. When Alma Dean was through with the combing out, she picked up a can and sprayed its contents all around Mrs. Burgess's head. Then she gave her back her glasses, along with the ever-present mirror. I watched the ritual repeated I'd seen the week before. Then Mrs. Burgess left.

Now it was just the two of us.

"Come over here and sit," she said.

I plumped myself down in the green vinyl chair in front of the mirror and rested my elbows on the chrome arms. Alma Dean looked at my reflection rather than at the real me. She studied it, occasionally lifting my hair to feel its texture, or gathering it in a wad in back so that it was just my head, skinned, with the ears showing.

"What brought this on?" she asked, like a doctor inquiring about the onset of symptoms.

"I just decided it was time," I answered.

"Big decision."

"Yeah," I said.

"Does Ruth know?"

My eyes dropped before I could command them not to. I shook my head. I waited for her sermon, but it didn't come.

"Well, let's move over there to the sink and I'll give you a shampoo first. I like to cut hair when it's wet."

By the time the shampoo and rinse were done, I was as limp as an old carrot. Alma Dean had me sit up while she squeezed my hair dry with a towel. "Now come back to the mirror," she ordered, "and we'll talk about how to style it."

With the towel turban wrapped around my head, I moved once more. When she removed the towel, the long strands dripped down my back, dampening my shirt.

"You know," she began, "that I can't cut it to look like your mom's."

"I wouldn't want you to. That would look funny on me."

She smiled. "You're right. It would. You have high cheekbones, broad forehead, straight nose—dramatic, really."

I stared at myself, trying to see what she saw. Dramatic is about the last word in the dictionary I'd use to describe myself.

"Of course," she went on, "if the hairstyle doesn't fit the personality, it looks like something added on, or the wrong size of clothes or something."

"I don't want to call attention to myself," I mumbled.

"Well, the very fact that you're getting it cut is going to attract a certain amount of attention," she reminded me as she rummaged among the doodads on the table in front of me. "Are you hoping to get boys to notice you more?"

Stunned by the blunt question, I couldn't say a word, but Alma Dean nodded as though her question had been answered anyhow.

She began to brush my hair in long, even strokes. By the time she'd gotten out all the tangles, it was nearly dry. Then she took up its length in her left hand and the scissors in her right, and in a few clean snips just below shoulder level she separated it and me from each other.

Alma Dean telephoned Mama to come for me. At six-thirty, when I stepped out onto the beauty shop porch and breathed the cold night air, I realized that I'd somehow gotten used to the mix of aromas inside. I felt the prickles of hair under my collar. The strange sweet-smelling softness of my own hair brushed my cheeks. Despite the cold, I wouldn't put my cap on. Instead I reached up and touched the unfamiliar fluff.

Soon, instead of the familiar *putt-putt* of the VW, I recognized the distinctive throb of Uncle Tate's pickup. For a moment, I considered diving out of sight under Alma Dean's porch, but even while I was thinking about it, the truck turned off the highway into Alma Dean's yard. The headlights went off, the door on the driver's side swung open, and Uncle Tate jumped out, already striding before he hit the ground, but not toward me.

"Here I am!" I shouted, running to head him off.

"I see you!" he said, never stopping.

"Well, I'm ready to go home!" I grabbed at his coat sleeve, but he ignored me as though I was no more than a pesky fly. He gained the porch and banged on the door with his fist. I was beside him in a second.

"What're you *doing*, Uncle Tate? She's closed for the night—"

But of course she opened the door, as who wouldn't if somebody was knocking your house down. The hall light shone fully on her.

Between the time I'd walked out and now, she'd changed from her polyester smock into a blue satiny-looking housecoat. Was, in fact, still knotting its sash in front as she opened the door. The robe fitted her like skin, moving as she moved. When it caught the light it appeared to flash and wink with an energy of its own.

"Yes?" she said, entirely cool.

"I'm Tate Field," he said in a kind of strangled voice. His eyes strayed to the robe, where it lapped over her bosom. "This girl's uncle." He gestured toward me but never looked in my direction.

Alma Dean smiled. "Of course. You're Ruth's brother. I remember you from years ago. What can I do for you?"

Now he raised his eyes to hers. "This girl's hair is cut off!"

"So it is!" she replied, as though it was the first time she'd noticed. If I hadn't been so scared and embarrassed, I would have laughed. "Doesn't it look fine?"

"It's an abomination!" he shot back. But he still hadn't looked at me, so how could he know? "What right do you have, cutting off her hair without anybody's permission?"

"Why, I had her permission," Alma Dean said, still cordial. "I wasn't aware that I had to have anyone else's. She *is* eighteen." She unhooked the screen door and pushed it open a bit. "Would you like to come inside and talk about it?"

Uncle Tate took a full step backward. "Get in the truck, Missy!"

I opened my mouth to apologize, but one look from Alma Dean cleared me of that responsibility. "G'd night," I mumbled. "Thanks for everything."

"Good night, Missy," she said kindly. "I'll talk to you later."

"Not if I have anything to say about it!" Uncle Tate raved. Alma Dean shut the front door and in a moment the porch light went out.

I sat in the truck shivering and mad as Uncle Tate turned it around and headed toward home. He muttered under his breath some of his favorite words, such as abomination, Satan's work, and judgment.

Other than that, though, he was strangely quiet, like someone in shock.

As soon as the truck stopped in our yard, I was out of it like a flash. The front door opened before I could turn the knob. Mama stood just inside, waiting. Her whole face lit up when she saw me.

"Missy! You look gorgeous!" She grabbed me, coat and all, then held me away from her to get a better look. "Just gorgeous. Alma Dean—"

But she got no further, because Uncle Tate was close on my heels.

"Ruth, this is *it!*" he exclaimed, wild-eyed. He pulled off Grampa's hat and more or less threw it on the hat tree by the door.

"Go upstairs and put up your things," Mama said to me. "I'll have your supper on the table when you get back."

"That woman is an agent of the devil, Ruth!"

"What on earth are you talking about?"

"I'll tell you what I'm talking about—" His voice faded to a muffled murmur as he followed Mama back to the kitchen and I escaped to my room. I shut the door to block out his voice, turned on the light, and went straight to the mirror.

There I was, but oh so different from when I'd left this morning. It was me and not me. My clothes were the same, my face was the same. And yet in some impossible-to-turn-back way, I was changed. Automatically, I reached for the hairbrush, then realized as I raised it to my head that the usual two strokes left, two strokes right wouldn't work anymore. Carefully, I gave the new do a few tentative pats to neaten the wisps blown loose by the wind.

I could hardly get enough of looking.

"Missy!" Mama called from below. "Your dinner's getting cold."

Startled and a little ashamed, I threw the brush on the bed and hurried downstairs to the kitchen. Gramma, just emptying the dishwater from the sink, glanced up at me and did a double take.

"My stars!" she said, pressing one wet hand to her cheek.

"Aw, Gramma. It's not that bad, is it?"

"Who said anything about bad?" She sniffed, recovering herself.

Mama and Uncle Tate had already eaten, but they sat at the table. I pulled out my chair and sat down, braced for whatever would come.

"We didn't know where you were, Missy," said Mama.

"I know. I'm sorry. I'll never do that again, I promise." I took a bite of biscuit. "Jim and I were going to the dock when school was out, but he had to stay in and we got started late. Then I just decided to do . . . this . . . on the spur of the moment."

"You and Jim again, huh?" Uncle Tate nodded as though it was just what he expected. "It's all connected."

"Tate, I told you I'd handle this." Mama's voice carried the weight of something that must have passed between them while I was upstairs.

"Jim's been helping me with a . . . problem," I explained. "I asked him to take me to Alma Dean's."

"You could've at least called when you got there," Gramma spoke up, slamming a cabinet door to punctuate the sentence.

"I know, but I was afraid I'd lose my nerve if I didn't go right ahead with my plan."

"That woman talked you into it, didn't she?" Gramma said.

"No, she didn't." I felt calm. "It was my idea, and I had plenty of time to think it over, in case I wanted to change my mind."

Uncle Tate pushed back from the table and stood up suddenly. He marched himself off to the living room and turned on the TV loud enough to be heard in the front yard.

Mama put her hands over her ears and shook her head. *"Now* what?"

"His feelings are hurt," Gramma said, coming over to sit in Uncle Tate's chair. "He was just trying to help. You ought to be glad he feels responsible for Missy."

"He doesn't have to," Mama said. "It's fine for him to care what happens to her, but he's not her daddy. And he's not Pa. *I'm* responsible."

"Hey!" I said. "What about me? *I'm* responsible."

Mama nodded. "That's right. And I'm glad you feel that way about it."

"Are you mad that I didn't tell you before I had my hair cut?"

"Of course not! It's your hair—and you look terrific."

I smiled, relieved. "How about you, Gramma. Do you like it?"

"It looks all right, I guess," she said grudgingly. "But I'll tell you what I don't like." She leaned forward and her eyes narrowed behind the glasses. "I don't like this fraternizing with Alma Dean Slater."

"Rodriguez," I said automatically.

"Whatever! She's a bad influence, that's what she is. Why'd she have to come back here anyhow is what I want to know?"

"She came back to take care of her mother," Mama answered. "She gave up a successful business in Charlotte to do it, too."

"Hmmph!" Gramma didn't like to think that Alma Dean's motives might be other than self-serving. It ruined her argument.

"Look," said Mama, also leaning forward until their noses were only inches apart, "you've hardly spoken two words to Alma Dean since she came back. You're still going by what you thought of her years ago. Give her a chance, Ma. She's a great person."

Gramma leaned away from her. "With a face knee-deep in makeup and hair changing color every day? Hmmph!"

"That's her advertising, Ma. It's better than a billboard. You don't need to worry about me overdoing the makeup or changing my hair color. Even if I wanted to, Alma Dean would talk me out of it, I'm sure."

"Me either, Gramma," I chimed in. "Getting my hair cut will last me for a while."

"I doubt that," she said, giving me a sour look. She got up from the table. "I'm going to watch TV. Wash your dishes when you get done."

When Gramma was out of earshot, Mama said, "Was Tate awful?"

"Pretty awful."

Mama sighed. "Well, at least I've told Alma Dean enough Tate stories she wouldn't be bowled over."

"*He* was the one bowled over," I said. "He said some insulting things, but to tell the truth, I don't think if you asked him, he could tell you what he said. It was like his mouth got disconnected from his brain when he saw her."

Mama looked thoughtful. "Is that so?" While I finished eating, she propped her chin on one hand and gazed at me, but I think she had her mind on something else.

Chapter 9

I stood minus my cap in the biting wind and waited for the bus. In a funny sort of way I was reminded of the time I bought plastic fangs for Halloween and wore them to breakfast. No one had noticed at first. I had thought, for a few horrible seconds, that even with fangs, I looked no different than usual. But then Gramps looked up and the shock on his face was totally satisfying.

So maybe now I exaggerated the effect of the haircut on my looks. Maybe all I'd get would be some mildly puzzled stares, as people tried to figure out what was wrong or different.

I missed the warmth of the wool hat. I was ashamed of the vanity that kept me from putting it on, but not ashamed enough. From time to time, I pressed my mittened hands over my ears or covered my nose, ever conscious of the curtain of hair on either side of my face.

It seemed forever before the bus finally stopped at our mailbox, but actually it was right on time. The door opened with its accustomed squeal and I looked up into Tawanda's face to read there what she saw.

"A-law, girl!" she shrieked. "What you done to your hair?"

At that, almost the entire passenger load rose to its feet to see what she was talking about.

"Sit down, you monkeys!" she bellowed, then grinning broadly she put out her hand for the usual greeting. "Looks good. Looks *real* good!"

"Thanks." I ducked my head, relieved to have gotten it over with. Only I reckoned without the mixture of groans, squeals, and whistles from the others. The bus sounded like a barnyard.

"Cut it out!" I hollered, and everybody laughed. The motion of the bus rocked me backward into the seat as Tawanda revved the engine and headed toward school.

"You don't look like yourself," Joey Harper said.

"Is that bad or good?" I asked him.

"It's good!" called a seventh grader from two seats away. His remark prompted more laughter.

"Y'all mind out back there!" Tawanda warned. Then to me she said, "Whoever did it's going to get some business outta that. You watch. Every white girl in school'll be wanting that hairdo."

"Aw, no, Tawanda. People don't copy me."

"You watch," she said again.

By the time we arrived at school, I was more than happy

for the senior privilege of getting off the bus first. Looking neither right nor left, I headed straight for the side door, hoping to get to the girls' bathroom unnoticed. I needed to see a mirror for a reminder of the self I'd be carrying around all day.

But Sue's little red Honda careened into the senior parking lot directly in front of me. She parked and waved and rolled down the window all at the same time.

"Missy!" she screamed, pretending to faint. "My God!"

The door opened and she tumbled out, grabbing at books, purse, keys.

"Calm down," I said, flustered by her extreme behavior. "Or I won't walk with you."

But Sue bubbled on, exclaiming and touching as if she'd never seen a haircut before. By the time we got inside the building, I was ready to go back home and hide under the sofa.

"I'm going in here," I mumbled, ducking into the bathroom. But I couldn't lose her. Under the fluorescent strip light, the long mirror over the lavatories reflected me looking at Sue looking at me.

"What's wrong?" I asked.

"Wrong? Nothing's wrong. I just think you look wonderful! Who cut it for you?"

The question held weight. I am not used to this kind of conversation, where what is said is not what is meant.

"Mrs. Rodriguez."

"Really? You wouldn't think—" She stopped before the words came out, but I had a pretty good idea what they would have been. Sue goes to Elizabeth City to have

85

her hair styled. "Well," she went on, "you aren't going to have any trouble getting a date for the JanDance *now*."

It was what I wanted to hear, and yet it made me mad. Nothing about me—the real me—was different. What did I care about any boy who looked only at outside appearances? At the same time, to be honest, why had I bothered if this wasn't exactly what I'd hoped for?

I closed my eyes tight, squinting them shut to blot out Sue, myself, the girls' bathroom swarming with morning people touching up hairdos and lipstick. I turned away from the mirror before opening them again.

"I've got to see Ms. Hollins before class," I told her, already striding in hopes of leaving her behind. "I'll see you after a while."

"You know that boy from Elizabeth City I told you about?" she called at my back. "He's six-two and a basketball player."

I pretended I hadn't heard. It was going to be a long day.

With so many people jamming the hallways just before first bell, nobody pays much attention to anyone else. I had a minute or two of peace while I opened my locker, put in it the books I wouldn't need, and took out the ones I would. I thought about a Funky Winkerbean cartoon I'd seen where Crazy stays in his locker, and then I imagined my tall self spending the day in there folded up out of sight among the books and stinky gym shoes. The notion struck me funny and I snorted.

"What's so funny?" asked a familiar voice.

I slammed the locker and turned, all in a single motion. "You had to be there," I said.

"Oh, Lord!" said Jim, in something between a gasp and a groan.

"See what happens when you let people off in front of beauty shops," I said, joking because I was afraid to hear what he thought.

"I didn't even know it was you," he said, still staring. "I heard a snort that sounded like you—"

"It's me," I said.

Jim was truly stunned, to the point where I feared a slap on the cheek might be the only thing that would bring him around.

"Come *on*," I said. "Quit it!"

He sort of shook his head and blinked. "That's enough," he said.

"Enough what?"

"Just don't do anything else."

This had to be the weirdest conversation I'd ever carried on, and the worst of it was that Jim was serious. The bell rang just then.

"I've got to go," I said.

"Me, too."

But neither of us made a move.

"You're gonna be late," he told me, reaching out to give me a little shove toward homeroom.

"I'm going, I'm going," I said testily. I started to add "See you at lunch," but then I remembered yesterday afternoon. He had a lot of making up to do with Melanie. I didn't need to be around. "See you sometime."

He waited until I got to the door of the room. Then he said. "You look pretty."

My face flamed. The room tilted. I don't really remember how I got to my seat.

You look pretty.

I could hear Jim's voice in my ears, his soft drawl like a ghost echo from a dream.

How could a person feel so distressed and pleased at the same time? I was vaguely aware of Sue draped over the back of her desk onto mine, grinning like I was something she'd produced in art class.

I looked down and saw my big hands and not-so-clean fingernails, my old army jacket and jeans. It was the same body as always, a reassurance in a discouraging sort of way. I kept my eyes focused downward while Mr. Preston checked the roll. I didn't want anyone looking at me. I didn't want to have to answer to anyone's smart remarks. Mr. Preston's strictness about classroom conduct was a blessing for the moment; nobody could say anything to me without getting in trouble.

A wad of paper bounced on my desk, right under my nose. I glanced up, caught Chuck grinning and pointing for me to open it. I did, taking care to hold it below the desktop so Mr. Preston wouldn't see.

I thought we had a new student, the note read. *Do we?* I frowned at him.

"Missy?" Mr. Preston said. "It is Missy?" He peered at me, took off his glasses, put them back on. I slouched farther down in the desk, hard to do because of my long legs.

"Yessir," I mumbled.

I'll give him credit, Mr. Preston has more sensitivity than most teachers. He caught my drift. Immediately he was all business again, asking for absentee excuses, taking up money for some books he'd ordered for us, and announcing that the senior class would have a brief but important meeting in the auditorium during activity period.

But others craned their necks to see why he had paid attention to me. It was a slow-passing fifteen minutes. When the first-period bell finally rang, I was already tired and classes hadn't even begun. I wished that I was at Cedar Bay again, at the end of the longest pier. Yesterday Jim and I had stood beside the rail and watched the setting sun.

This morning, he'd said, *Just don't do anything else.*

And, *You look pretty.*

So it's true, then, that I, like Mama, will go under in a shot. People have been telling me for years that I'm smart, I'm dependable, I'm ambitious, I'm bound to succeed. But none of those has made my knees buckle or my brain turn to mush.

At the beginning of activity period, all of us in the senior class piled into the auditorium. Only one side of the double auditorium door was open, which is why Melanie and I ended up trying to squeeze through at the same time. Our shoulders bumped and we both said *Excuse me* before we realized who the other person was.

"Well, look at you!" Melanie said. She didn't crack a smile.

"No, don't." I tried to make a joke of it. "People've been looking at me all morning. I feel like putting a sack over my head."

"It's very nice."

"Thanks," I muttered.

About that time Sue came along and grabbed me by the arm. "Come on and sit by me," she ordered, pulling me down the slanting aisle. "We *have* to talk!"

Melanie disappeared from my view. I figured she'd gone to sit with Jim. I made myself not look.

Sue loves to sit near the front anywhere she goes. We ended up in the third row from the front, where the rest of the class could look at the backs of our heads.

"His name is Winston Harte," she said, starting right in. "He's a hunk."

"Whose name?"

"The boy I've been telling you about all this time!"

"Sue, why don't *you* ask him—you're the one wants him here so bad."

She looked at me as though I might be the world's dumbest female. "I've already been *asked*, Missy. I can't go with more than one person."

"Tell me," I said, "if Winston Harte is such a hunk, why would he want to come out here in the country to a dance with somebody he's never laid eyes on? It doesn't make any sense. What have you told him?"

Sue skipped lightly over the main points and said, "Well, if he saw a picture of you right now, I wouldn't have to say anything. He'd see for himself."

"I guess you think nobody here will ask me," I said.

Caught off guard, she opened her mouth partway, closed it, opened it again with a little half-breath. "I never said that. Just—nobody has, in the past."

"How do you know?"

"Well . . . I mean . . . if they had, you'd've had dates!" The words rushed out, about half an octave above her usual vocal range. By now everyone around us was privy to the conversation.

"Maybe I said no," I mumbled, not expecting her to believe me, but feeling some satisfaction in introducing the idea to her limited experience.

The class advisors began calling for order, so we had to hush. With half an ear, I listened while Mrs. Seabright outlined the direction of our lives for the next five months. Why had I ever thought that "senior" was a synonym for "freedom?" In exchange for our few privileges, we became hostages to a long list of calendar dates and deadlines. I was also beginning to find out how expensive it was to be graduating. Every time I turned around, I needed money for something at school. With a sigh, I closed my eyes. I saw us in our caps and gowns being spewed out from a kind of giant meat grinder onto the auditorium stage while Mrs. Seabright held our diplomas just out of reach. Meanwhile, some of us had other deadlines to meet—interviews and campus visits, tests, papers, and after-school jobs. Suddenly I longed to be an eighth grader again, still four years removed from Life with a capital L. I opened my eyes just as Mrs. Seabright came to the end of her list and dismissed us.

Sue and I walked out of the auditorium together.

"Well," she said, "do you want me to have Winston call you?"

"Thanks," I said, "but I think I'll pass up Winston. Nothing against him—or you."

Her look told me I was making a big mistake, but she didn't nag. "Just let me know if you change your mind," she said as we parted ways.

I wasn't going to change my mind. This year—my last at Wyndham—I was going to hold out for being an ask*ee*. If it didn't happen, I'd go to the JanDance alone as I've always done.

But who would ask me?

I walked faster to get away from the question.

Chapter 10

The children were just waking up from their naps when I slipped in through the side door of the day-care center and hung my jacket in the closet beside the brooms and mops. I dropped my bookbag on the closet floor and went into Mrs. Tilley's office to sign in.

Mrs. Tilley battles a tendency to plumpness, both by dieting and by wearing clothes a size too small. Personally, I like her size and so do the kids. She has a soft lap. She sat at her desk writing. Mrs. Tilley has even more paperwork to do that Ms. Hollins. I often hear her muttering about the Federal Government.

"I'm here," I said, scribbling my initials on the clipboard sheet. I started out the door so as not to interrupt her, but she looked up.

"Whoa!" she called out. "Come back here."

I backtracked obediently, wondering what deed I'd left undone.

"Wow!" she exclaimed. She got up from her desk and came over to touch my hair. Lots of people had touched it today, like maybe they weren't sure it was my real hair. "When did you do that?"

"Last night."

"Well, don't be so apologetic, for goodness sakes! You look terrific. Who in the world styled it for you?"

"Mrs. Rodriguez."

"Alma Dean did that? My goodness, I never knew she—" Mrs. Tilley stopped, then frowned slightly. "She does my hair, too."

Mrs. Tilley's hair is a steady brown, a shade not natural to women her age. She wears it teased and swooped. I've always accepted her hairdo as part of her, but now I thought about what Tawanda said that morning on the bus. What if everybody started asking Alma Dean to fix their hair like mine? A picture of Mrs. Tilley with my hairdo came to mind, followed closely by a picture of me with hers. It took all the politeness Mama ever taught me to keep a straight face.

"Well, I'd better get busy," I said, backing out of the office. "Jo probably needs my help."

My first duties when I come in afternoons are to help the kids potty, put their shoes and socks back on, and then bundle them up for outdoor play. That day, on the playground, I acted like a kid myself, racing around and shrieking and generally being boisterous. Jo Battle's look let me know she thought I was being too silly, but I pretended not to notice. When we finally came back inside, panting and warm, I felt almost like my old self.

Mrs. Tilley met us in the cramped hallway. "You had a phone call, Missy."

Immediately I thought *emergency*. "Was it Mama?" I asked, unzipping my jacket. "Is something wrong at home?"

"Calm down," she said, her half-smile suggesting things. "It was a male. He left a number for you to call. It's here somewhere."

I stood beside her desk while she scrounged among the papers. "Here we go," she said, uncovering it at last. I took the pink slip and recognized the number right away. But I pretended not to.

"Thanks," I said, tucking it into my jeans pocket.

"Don't you want to use the phone?"

"Not right now, thanks." I walked out of the office, feeling her eyes on my back. The slip of paper crackled in my pocket.

The number was Jim's.

What could possibly be important enough for Jim to call me at work? The more I thought about it, the more nervous I became. I imagined myself in his place and concluded that only something major would prompt him to do such a thing, maybe some kind of trouble. When Betty Allen started the afternoon story hour, I went back to the office to use the phone. With Mrs. Tilley sitting right there.

I dialled the number and prepared myself for one of the Perkins kids and the usual hollering contest.

"Hello." Unmistakably Jim, breathless, as though he'd run to get there first.

"It's Missy," I said. "Did you call me?"

"Sure did. How're you getting home after work?"

"Mama, same as usual. Why?"

"Call her and tell her you got another ride," he said. "I'll pick you up."

"What's this all about?"

"Can't tell you now. But I really need to talk to you."

I hesitated, almost said no. But this was Jim. He wouldn't say no to me if I needed him. "I can't be late for dinner," I said, stalling.

"I promise I'll have you home by six-thirty," he said. "Please."

Something in his voice did things to my knees. "Okay," I said. "I usually get through here about five-forty. I'll meet you out front."

I called Mama and, without mentioning any names, told her I had another ride and would be home by six-thirty. She didn't ask any questions, for which I was grateful since Mrs. Tilley's ears were practically cupping by themselves in order to hear better.

"Thanks," I said over my shoulder, as I went out. I slipped back into the classroom where Betty told a story with motions to the three- and four-year olds. I got down on the floor beside Perry and took up the motion of the moment, which was lap-slapping to imitate the sound of running feet.

". . . and the man ran as fa-a-a-st as he could from the bear," Betty said.

"Yeah!" said Perry. Biting his lip with concentration, he worked hard to make his hands move as fast as running feet, not an easy task for somebody only three.

We careened through the rest of the story as the bear chased the man through a tunnel, up and down a hill, around a house, and over a bridge. When the man was safely home, Perry collapsed backward on the carpet with a loud, satisfied sigh. I tickled his stomach and he giggled, looking up at me from the floor.

Immediately he rolled over and sat up with a frown. "Where'd your hair go?"

I shrugged, turning empty palms out. "Last I saw, it was on the floor at the beauty shop."

He got to his feet and reached to touch what was left with a timid finger. "It was the longest hair in the world," he said.

"Well, maybe the longest *you'd* ever seen," I said.

"I wish I had it," he said unexpectedly. "Did the lady sweep it up and put it in a bag?"

"You mean the hair? I think she just threw it in the trash." I was curious. "What would you do with it, Perry?"

"I might keep it in a treasure box," he said, very serious. "Or I might paste it on me and make it hang down long." He bent over, touching his toes to show me. "It would cover me up."

"Perry, you beat all!" I said, laughing. Only half joking, I asked, "Are we still friends?"

"Yes," he said with absolute certainty, falling into my lap and snuggling close. He stuck his thumb in his mouth.

"Hey!" Jo said from the other side of the room. "Perry, let Missy up from there. She's got to help me."

"Yeah, yeah!" Two other children rushed over and hurled themselves at me. I found myself smothered in arms and giggles.

Jim was waiting in the truck with the engine running when I came out of the center. I opened the door and climbed in, trying to remember and imitate my former matter-of-fact self.

"Where're we going?" I asked, when he turned the truck around and headed down the highway away from home. "Don't forget, I have to be back by six-thirty."

"I promised, didn't I?"

He hadn't answered the question, but to ask again sounded too much like nagging. I focused instead on the far edge of the beam cast by the headlights and waited for what would come next.

"I guess you wonder what this is about," he said, not even leading up to it.

"I guess I do. Are you telling?"

"Look, don't *you* get smart with me, too," he said in such a despairing tone that I abandoned all games on the spot. "Melanie's really mad at me."

"You mean about yesterday afternoon? Didn't you explain it to her?"

"Sure I did, but she doesn't believe I'm telling the truth." He drummed the steering wheel with his open hand. "I told her you'd asked my advice."

"Well, that's the truth," I said, "only, I hope you didn't give details."

"I didn't. I told her you'd asked my opinion on something last week, and that I'd thought of some more stuff to say and made plans to take you home after school yesterday so I could say it."

"And I bet *she* said, 'Well, if that's all there was to it, why didn't you tell me ahead of time instead of letting me make a fool of myself waiting around for a ride home?' "

Jim turned quickly to look at me. The truck veered over the center line. "How'd you know? Did she tell you already?"

"Keep your eyes on the road," I said. "No. I just guessed."

"I said I didn't much like her lying in wait for me like that," he said. "Then she really *did* get mad. I guess I shouldn't have said it."

I eyed the speedometer. "You're going too fast. We're almost to Milway."

Obediently, he took his foot off the accelerator and the truck slowed. I felt sorry for him, but I could see Melanie's side of things, too. I remembered her cold glare in the auditorium.

"What do you want me to do?" I asked.

"Help me figure out what to say to her, I guess, so she'll believe me."

The tires whined along the highway in a gray, one-note song. So many things I wanted to say. "Jim, she wouldn't believe me either. She'd figure that if you had something to hide, I would, too."

"But we don't!" he burst out. "That's just it. Why can't she accept that?"

I shrugged. Jim isn't used to being disbelieved. Maybe,

until Melanie, he'd never had to deal with hidden meanings and such. "She's never felt right about me," I told him. "I think she's always believed we were more than friends, so the least little thing makes her suspicious."

"You're kidding!" said Jim. "Why would she think that?"

The sign announcing MILWAY appeared around the next curve, and right next to it Snug Cartwright's store. Jim pulled into the lighted parking lot beside the store. A neon Pepsi sign flickered in the window. He set the parking brake and then leaned back to look at me.

"Well," I said, "what if it was the other way around? What if she and, say, Beeny Taylor had always been good friends. And what if, even after you and she started dating, she still had private conversations or went places with him and you were sort of left out. How'd you feel?"

He shifted in the seat, propped a knee against the steering wheel, stared out the window into the night. "If she told me they were just friends, I'd believe her." He paused. "I think."

In the light from the store, his face was a study as he appeared to backtrack and look at everything that had happened from this new point of view. Finally he said, "I guess when you don't feel guilty, you don't go around trying to cover up."

I smiled and shook my head, amazed, but glad in a way that there was somebody like that still alive in the world. "Well, if you want me to make some kind of sworn statement to save your skin, I'll do it."

He studied me, the way I've seen him look at a boat he might buy. I stood it for about a minute.

100

"Take it or leave it," I said in a mock-tough tone of voice, looking at my watch. "Time's passing. We've got to head back."

"No," he said, slow and dreamy, like somebody waking up from a deep sleep.

"But you promised!" I sat up, alarmed, all set to take the wheel.

"Not that," he said testily. He, too, sat up, and started the engine. "I mean I don't need a sworn statement. I'll handle it myself."

"That's good. I didn't really want to do it anyway, but I would, for you."

My own words echoed in my ears and I felt suddenly peculiar. He might mistake my meaning. In a kind of wild desperation, I started chattering as we sped up the highway about whatever came to mind, which in this case happened to be college, how much I was looking forward to it, how hopeful my prospects were, now that Mama was 100 percent behind me.

"Good." His flat voice stopped me cold.

"Pardon me," I mumbled. "Guess I got off the subject." I looked out the window on my side, feeling both embarrassed and resentful and not sure why.

"Who're you going to the JanDance with?" he asked.

My head swivelled. I didn't think I'd heard right. I just sat there kind of staring at him.

"Well?" he prompted.

"Myself, as usual," I said. "Sue's been trying to get me to go with some dude she knows in Elizabeth City. I told her no."

"Why?"

I folded my arms across my chest and pushed back against the seat. "Because I don't want to!" I snapped. "And I've got only eight minutes to get home or I'm grounded for life!"

We made it back to my house with no more meaningful conversation and a minute to spare. I had the door open almost before the truck came to a full stop in our yard.

"Thanks for your help," he said. I listened for sarcasm, but it wasn't there.

"Whatever," I said. "I hope you and Melanie get . . . get straightened out." I slammed the door and hurried toward the lighted porch, aware that the truck stayed right there until I turned the knob and went inside.

Chapter 11

"Missy, is that you?" Mama called from the dining room when I came in the back door. Her voice sounded strained and my heart sank.

"It's about time," Uncle Tate declared as I pulled out my chair and sat down at the table. "How many more evenings are you planning to come in late?"

"No more," I said.

"Have some ham," said Mama, passing me the platter. "The beans and potatoes are right there by your plate."

I helped myself, aware that Gramma and Uncle Tate at least were expecting me to volunteer where I'd been and with whom. But my teeth were firmly clenched.

"Are you and that boy planning to elope or something?" Uncle Tate said suddenly.

My head jerked up.

Clearly pleased with the effect, he bulldozed ahead. "Well, you been seeing him off and on now for nearly two weeks. Only he's never once been here and called for you or spoke to us."

I laid my fork carefully on the plate, measuring words. "Uncle Tate, for the last time: Jim is my good friend. He has a girlfriend, a person he dates, and it's not me. We've been pals since we were little kids. That's all."

"That's what you say." He pointed his knife at me. "But a boy that age doesn't have a girl for a best friend, or vicey versey. There's hanky-panky mixed up in all this, I'll bet my last dollar."

"Stop it, Tate!" Mama's fist came down hard on the table. Dishes jumped. So did the rest of us.

She stood up, propping the knuckles of both hands on the table and leaning forward on them like a speaker at the PTA.

"There are a lot of things I could say to you, Tate Fields, some of which don't have anything to do with the matter at hand. Such as, why is a grown man going on fifty living with his mama, and where does he get the right to play dictator to his niece who was doing just fine before he came two months ago! But I won't dwell on those things at this point."

"Now wait—" Uncle Tate began.

Mama's right hand came up, her index finger pointing straight as a spear. "You wait. I've tolerated your mess for Ma's sake, but now you've gone too far. You'll never meet another kid as good as Missy. She's never given me or anybody else cause to worry about her, and yet you treat her like she was some juvenile delinquent. You haven't even tried to see her the way she really is. You're just making her fit your preconceived notions. And what I have to say to you is, either you quit it or get out!"

"Ruth!" Gramma leaped into the fray. "This is *my* house. I'm the one to say who leaves and who stays."

Mama didn't miss a beat. "All right, then, it's either him or Missy and me. You can decide which, Ma, because for sure we're not living in the same house with him acting the way he does!"

She sat down then, breathing hard. I felt like I was in a dream.

Gramma's hand went to her chest, pressing there nervously. Her mouth twitched when she tried to talk. "Ruth, I know you don't mean that. Once you've had a chance to think about it—"

"No, ma'am," Mama interrupted, shaking her head for emphasis. "I can't think of anything I'd take back."

"But you've got nowhere else to go," said Gramma.

Mama shrugged, like it wasn't any great concern. "I'll manage."

Uncle Tate sat like a man struck by lightning. I don't suppose he ever expected his little sister to rise up like that.

As for me, I cried. I cried for the confusion I was feeling and for all the contention I'd stirred up in the family just by being here. Once I got started, I couldn't stop. I leaned my head on my hands and wept into the plate of ham and vegetables. I mopped my cheeks with a paper napkin and sobbed aloud.

Mama was beside me in a second, putting her arm around me and holding me close. "It's all right, Missy," she said, over and over.

"See there, you've gone and got her upset," Gramma said, to no one in particular. "I declare, I don't know what things are coming to!"

Uncle Tate looked glumly at his plate and didn't say anything. His expression wavered between regret and shock, like a kid's whose mischief has gotten out of hand.

I didn't help with the cleaning up after dinner. Mama sent me to take a hot shower. Under the stream of water, the scene I'd just witnessed began to sink in.

I see Mama and me standing out beside the mailbox in the cold, waiting for the Trailways with our shabby suitcases and a couple of boxes. Uncle Tate is on the porch wearing Grampa's hat and a smug smile, saying *Good riddance*. Gramma isn't in the scene. She is probably back in the kitchen cooking and wishing the trouble would blow over.

But how was she going to be able to choose between her two children, not to mention her only grandchild? Maybe she'd have to run us all off, to get any peace of mind.

I finished drying off and put on my pajamas and bathrobe. I felt a lot better. The cry and the shower had cleaned me out. In spite of a stuffy head and puffy eyes, my nerves weren't humming anymore and the throat lump had disappeared. I'd put away crying a long time ago. I thought I was Mature. Now, as I went along the hall to my room, I wondered if I should resort to tears more often.

Mama sat on my bed waiting for me.

"I'm really okay," I said before she could ask the question. "I don't know what came over me."

"It's probably time for your period," she said as she always does. When I opened my mouth to deny it, she kept on. "But there's more to it. What's this thing about Jim?"

I sat down on the other side of the bed. "It's not really *about* Jim," I said slowly. Or at least it hadn't started out being about Jim, but I was reluctant to say that. "I . . . well, you know the night I met him up at the store? It was to ask his advice about something, friend to friend."

"And did he give it?"

"He didn't know what I was talking about, not until he'd had time to think it over, which took a few days."

I told her about his plan to bring me home Monday afternoon and what had happened with Melanie. "Now he's in bad with her," I finished, "and it's so dumb! She thinks—"

I stopped, choking on the words. Mama said them for me.

"She thinks you and Jim have a thing going on."

"I guess," I said, getting up to pace. "It's not true, but she's all set to believe it. She ought to know better. I mean, if there *was* anything, Jim and I would've been going together a long time ago. He . . . we were never interested in each other like that."

Mama just sat there, being quiet, looking thoughtful.

"Anyway," I said, "I appreciate your standing up for me like you did. But I don't want you to get in trouble with Gramma and Uncle Tate on my account."

"Don't you worry," Mama said. "I meant every word.

We don't have to put up with being treated like idiot doormats."

"It's all my fault." I sighed, sitting down on the bed again. "If I hadn't started this college business—"

Mama burst out laughing. "What a conceited thing to say, Missy! It isn't true, but even if it was, aren't you glad? *I* am!" She leaned toward me and covered my hand with hers. "I'm thirty-eight. That's still pretty young, you know. Thanks to you and Alma Dean, it has finally dawned on me that I don't have to live out my days in Tucker. I can go back to school and train for a better job. I've even been thinking that I could move to wherever you go to college, get an apartment and all. There are all sorts of possibilities, some I haven't even thought of yet."

She bubbled with eagerness, like somebody surrounded by heaps of unopened Christmas presents.

"You talk like Gramma'd rather have Uncle Tate around than us," I said. "What if she chooses the other way? We couldn't very well just take off and leave after that, could we?"

Mama's bright eagerness faded right before my eyes. When she spoke, her voice sounded flat. "*You* could. It's not us we're talking about, is it? You're leaving no matter what."

It was a funny-feeling moment. Mama got up. "We were talking about you and Jim," she said. "How'd we get off the subject?"

"Jim and Melanie," I corrected her mechanically. My mind was still on her strange reaction to what I had said.

"Oh, well—things'll work out." She sighed. "Get some

sleep, now." She gave me a distracted kiss on the forehead and went out.

I leaned back on my pillow and listened to her footsteps going downstairs. I imagined her down there in the living room with Uncle Tate and Gramma, awash in their hurt feelings. The thought came to me that she might be trying to get us thrown out, but then I dismissed it. She had said she wanted me to go to college and I believed her. I didn't think she would really leave Gramma alone to go live wherever I was in school.

I turned off the light and lay in the dark, thinking about Jim and Melanie, wondering what he would say to convince her that he was truly hers. Deep in the night, I dreamed I was a mile out on the bay, drifting in a boat with no motor or oars, and that Melanie and Jim walked along the shore arm in arm, ignoring my cries for help.

Chapter 12

Then, like a bolt from the blue, a letter came notifying me that, on the basis of an essay I'd written and submitted with my application, I was a semifinalist for a Mary I. Smithwick Scholarship at Moriah College. I was invited to spend a February weekend on the campus for interviews. The three winners would receive full four-year scholarships. The letter said lots of things about my outstanding record and so forth, but I am no fool. I knew the exact same letter had gone out to no-telling-how-many other seniors around the state. I'd be competing with the best, some from very large high schools with better course offerings than Wyndham. It's funny how a person can feel hopeless and hopeful at the same time, like when you're holding a lottery ticket and you know it could be the one, but probably isn't.

Mama, when she heard it, jumped up and down and screamed, then hugged me until I couldn't breathe. I tried to tone her down.

"But Mama, I haven't won anything yet. I still have to—"

"But don't you understand what it means to be selected?" she interrupted. "You're a top contender." She refused to be muzzled. "I'm *proud* of you!"

"If I was you, I wouldn't start countin' my chickens," Uncle Tate said from his easy chair. "There's many a slip 'twixt the cup and the lip."

"I know that," I said. "I'm not taking anything for granted."

"A person could let something like this go to her head," Gramma spoke up.

"I won't," I declared.

"I wish you would," Mama said. "It never hurt a person to claim her talents."

"Well, it can hurt when they go overboard," Gramma said severely, "and you of all people ought to know it!"

"That's not fair, Gramma," I said. "You always bring up the one mistake Mama ever made, like it's too big to overcome, no matter what she does. I for one wish you'd stop it!"

It was Gramma's turn to look shocked. "Seems like you're already getting too big for your britches," she said. "If that's what this college scholarship stuff does to a person, then I don't know." She threw up her hands and went back to her kitchen, muttering to herself. I waited for Uncle Tate's two-cents' worth, but to my surprise, he didn't say anything. I put it down to strategy. Maybe after Mama's blowup at the table last night, he was contriving to get *us* thrown out instead of him. He hummed a hymn and turned on the television.

Mama sighed a little. "You didn't have to do that," she said to me. "There's no use arguing with her. Anyway, it doesn't bother me like it used to."

As I climbed the stairs to study for next day's physics test, I wondered if that was true. I couldn't imagine what it would be like if Mama cut me down every time I turned around. Maybe, after all, it would be a good idea for her and me to move out.

At school next day, I got excused to go to Ms. Hollins's office during activity period. As usual, there was a line of full chairs outside her office door. I hung around until the student she'd been talking to came out, then I stationed myself where she could see me and waved the letter from Moriah high over my head, pointing to it with the other hand. Ms. Hollins rose from behind her desk and came to the outer office.

I handed the letter to her and watched her read it, watched her eyes widen and brighten, knew she wasn't putting on an act when she whooped loudly and grabbed me, to the amazement of the five students sitting there.

"I *knew* it!" she exclaimed. "Missy Cord, you're on the way to something big. And just think—you haven't even *heard* from State and Carolina—they may offer you something just as good. Then you'll have to make decisions. Poor you!"

I didn't have a chance to open my mouth. She turned

to the audience of three boys and two girls. "Now *this*," she said, pointing to me, "is what you ninth graders have to aspire to. You buckle down and get those grades up, and who knows—you might be bringing me a letter that says you've made it to the semifinals for a big college scholarship."

It was embarrassing for them and me. They shifted in their chairs and looked at each other sheepishly. When you're in the ninth grade, being a senior is light years in the future. College is almost in the next life.

"Uncle Tate says there's many a slip 'twixt the cup and the lip," I said.

"He's such a cheerful man, isn't he?" Ms. Hollins winked at me and handed back the letter. "Off you go— I have to see all these muffins before lunch. We'll talk about the interviews sometime soon, so you'll know what to expect."

I thanked her, folded the letter, and stuck it in my back pocket. Now that Ms. Hollins knew, I didn't feel like telling anybody else except maybe Jim. I looked up and down the hall, not really expecting to see him. Since Tuesday he'd been avoiding me, and I figured Melanie had told him to, as a condition of their making up. I wanted to show him the letter and watch his slow smile. But maybe he wouldn't smile. Maybe he wouldn't really care one way or the other.

The bell rang and the hall filled with bodies. I moved with the crowd to my locker.

"Well!" said a cold voice nearby. "I guess you got what you wanted, didn't you? I hope you're satisfied."

I looked around, mostly out of curiosity. I didn't think the words were for me. But they were. Melanie stood there, clutching a couple of heavy books in front of her like a shield. If looks could kill, somebody would have had to start planning my funeral.

"What did you say?"

"You don't have to pretend," she said. "I know what you've been up to."

The people closest to us, while continuing whatever they were doing, seemed suddenly attentive. I felt like I was in somebody else's life. In mine, we don't do stuff like this.

"I'm sorry, Melanie," I said, striving to sound civil. "I'm really not sure what you mean."

"You almost had me fooled," she said. "Like you've got everybody else around here fooled."

I had to get past her to go to class. "I have physics this period," I said, "and the bell's about to ring. Could we talk some other time?"

"What is there to talk about?" she said, stepping aside.

"Just to get things straight," I said. "You're wrong about Jim and me. He's told you that, and I'm telling you. Don't give him a hard time." I felt like the woman with the baby King Solomon was about to cut in two.

"So why did he break up with me, then?" Melanie spit out the words.

I stopped in my tracks and stared at her. The bell rang. People melted away. She and I, in the middle of the hallway, me gawking, her soft face tight with anger.

"When did he do that?" I finally managed to ask. It came out so thin she had to lean forward to hear me.

114

"I guess you can find out all about it from him," she said.

Maybe she could see my genuine shock. Plus the fact that I ignored the bell, which I have never done in my entire high school career. For the second time in less than five minutes, I felt misplaced. Probably my body was sitting in physics right now, starting the test.

The test.

"Oh, my God! I'm late!" I whirled around and sprinted up the hall, my heart pounding. Mr. Francis had already shut the door. On test days, he locks it as soon as the bell rings. Through the glass pane, I could see everyone already seated, looking toward the front. When I knocked, all eyes swivelled in my direction. I could have died.

"Well, Missy," Mr. Francis said, opening the door. "You decided to show up, I see. Where's your excuse?"

"I don't have one, sir," I mumbled. I thought about all the times I've sat safely at my desk and watched somebody else go through this. Mr. Francis's bald head gleamed. His little mustache twitched. He is my severest teacher. He takes no mess. He was put out with me; it showed in his eyes, but time was passing and if he didn't get the test underway, people wouldn't be able to finish before the next bell rang.

"Go to your seat," he said. "And come by to see me after school."

"Yes, sir." I went to my desk without meeting anyone's eyes. This was awful. If I came by after school, I'd miss the bus and have to walk home. But I didn't dare protest.

I don't know how I got through that test. For one thing, it was almost as hard as a final exam, although shorter.

For another, I couldn't keep my mind on it. Melanie's words kept floating around in my brain—*So why did he break up with me? So why did he break up with me?*

Why did he?

I was still working on the final problem, when the bell rang. Mr. Francis is very strict. He gives us one extra minute after the bell to wind up. Then we're supposed to put down our pencils and hand in what we've done or risk a zero. I nearly panicked. I've always finished in time to go over everything and correct any careless mistakes. This time I carried an incomplete paper and laid it on his desk.

"I'm sorry, Mr. Francis," I said. "I'll see you after school."

He nodded and took the paper. He's used to seeing people after school.

I didn't see Jim all day, but I found his name on the daily absentees list. So what did *that* mean? Jim doesn't love school, but he doesn't play hooky, either.

The door to Mr. Francis's room was open when I got there. He sat at his desk among piles of papers, wielding his red pencil like a paintbrush. I walked in and stood beside him until he'd gotten through with the paper he was grading and put a D at the top with a quick flourish. I winced. It wasn't my paper, but it could have been.

"Well," he said mildly, looking up at me, "you certainly surprised me this morning."

"I'm really sorry," I said.

"Where were you?"

"Out in the hall, in front of my locker."

116

"Didn't you hear the bell?"

"Well, I did—and I didn't. At the time, it just didn't sink in."

Mr. Francis frowned. "I don't understand. That doesn't sound like you."

"What it was . . . a person tried to argue with me. I was trying to get by them, and then they told me something that . . . shocked me so bad I just kind of forgot what I was supposed to be doing."

It was the truth, but even as I said it, I realized that telling something in such vague terms may not cut it with a science teacher.

Mr. Francis searched among his piles of papers and drew out one with my name on it. A large red C decorated the right corner. "You didn't do so well."

I looked down at the floor. "I studied hard, Mr. Francis. But I guess I couldn't concentrate."

"Would you like to take it over?"

Startled, I looked up. "Are you serious?"

"Of course. A test isn't supposed to trick people into making mistakes. It's supposed to indicate how much you've learned." He held up my paper. "I know you can do better than this. You can retake the test right now. I'll give you different problems, to be fair to the other students."

For the next hour, while he graded papers, I worked problems. This time, I knew I'd done better when I brought my paper to his desk. "Thanks, Mr. Francis," I said. "If I hadn't studied, I wouldn't have felt so bad about the C."

"You want to hang around while I grade it?" he asked.

"Well, maybe not. I have to get home." It was already after four and I knew, if I walked, it would be dark by the time I got there.

"All right, then." He dismissed me with a nod. "I'll see you tomorrow in class—on time."

Despite the fact that I had a five-mile hike ahead of me, I actually welcomed some time to myself to think about the day. Had Jim been absent because he couldn't face Melanie after breaking up with her? I still couldn't believe he'd done it. Maybe Melanie was mistaken. I went over and over our conversation, but nothing he'd said made me think he was planning to do such a thing.

A car approached and I stepped off the pavement onto the muddy shoulder. The wet grass and mud soaked my sneakers through. Before long, my feet would begin to get cold. I walked faster. Fifteen minutes per mile, I told myself. Then I'd be home before dark.

A short while later, I heard the whine of a car engine behind me, coming closer and closer. Then it slowed, and a horn honked at my back. I turned to see Mr. Francis rolling down the window of his tan Datsun.

"Why didn't you tell me you didn't have a way home?" he said crossly. "Get in the car."

I crossed the highway and got in. "I don't mind walking," I said, but I was shivering and already grateful for the car's warmth.

He sped up again, staring ahead into the fading light. "I thought you had a car. Most kids do, don't they? More student cars in the parking lot than faculty!"

"Well, that's because there are more students," I said. "But no, I don't have a car. That'll have to wait till I'm out of college."

He glanced sideways at me. "So where are you going?"

I told him where I'd applied, and about the semifinals at Moriah.

"What do you plan to be?" he wanted to know.

"People ask me that all the time," I said. "I never know what to say."

"Do you plan to come back to Tucker?"

I looked down at my mittened hands. "I don't know," I said cautiously. "It depends."

"On?"

Mr. Francis is almost as bad as Jim about keeping on with the questions when you'd just as soon not deal with them.

"On whether I can get a job around here, I suppose," I said.

He sighed. "That's not very likely. We've been losing our best young people steadily for the past twenty-five, thirty years. The bright ones like you don't ever come back. I'll tell you, I get discouraged sometimes, knowing I'm in the export business."

"It doesn't seem right," I said. "Tucker's a good place to live."

"Sure, if you don't have to worry about making a living."

"Are you saying that a college education is a one-way ticket out of here?" I laughed a little because I sort of hoped he'd deny it.

"That's exactly what I'm saying. I wish it weren't so."

"That's our house up ahead on the left," I said, relieved that the ride was almost over. His words had made me sad. "Just let me off at the edge of the road, please."

"Don't ever walk home from school again if you miss the bus," Mr. Francis said as I got out. "You come to me first. If I can't give you a ride, I'll find one for you—understand?"

"Yes, sir. Thanks again, for everything." I smiled at him. He smiled back, kind of uneasily because he isn't used to it. Then he drove on.

I stood there until I couldn't see the taillights anymore. Then I crossed over the footbridge into our yard, thinking about all the strangenesses of the day, one of the strangest being that Mr. Francis has a soft heart.

Chapter 13

Gramma was at the sewing machine when I came in. "Well, why'd you miss the bus *this* time?"

"I had to stay after school and take my physics test over," I said, pulling off my coat. "I didn't do very well on it the first time."

Red-and-green plaid wool moved in a straight line under the presser foot as the machine hummed in high gear, but Gramma's concentration didn't fool me for a minute. "That doesn't sound too good, you falling down on your schoolwork. You aren't slacking off on your studying, are you?"

"No, ma'am." I pulled one of the straight-backed chairs over and sat down. "You know I study every night till bedtime."

"I know you go off up to your room," she said dryly,

peering over her glasses at me. "You could be reading confession magazines for all I know."

I had to laugh. "Gramma, I've never read one of those in my life!"

"Well, you know what I mean." She stopped the sewing machine and pushed up the lever.

"What's that?" I asked, nodding at the colorful wool.

"You'd like to know, wouldn't you?" She half-smiled as she bit the threads. She held up the garment, a skirt. "I thought you might need something new to wear to that interview, and I've been saving this piece. Stand up and let me see if I've about got it right."

I obeyed, standing close to her while she held it against my waist. She looked up and down, measuring with her eyes. Gramma can make things for me that I never have to try on till they're done. They always fit perfectly.

I knew without asking that she was doing this to make peace, to let me know she forgave my sharp words of yesterday. I could see down through her hair to her scalp, pink as baby skin. I wanted to reach out and pat it, to let her know I loved her right on past all her crustiness and criticism.

"It's really pretty," I said. "And I thank you for going to the trouble."

"Hmph. It might not be in style. I don't know much about what the young people are wearing these days."

"Me, either," I said. "But it looks good to me. Maybe Mama'll lend me her dark green sweater to go with it— the one that's too big for her."

A smile glimmered at the corner of Gramma's mouth and she nodded. "Yep. That'll be just the ticket."

122

We'd gotten through a sticky moment without either of us bringing disgrace on ourselves.

"Tate got called back to work today," she volunteered, as she began putting away her sewing. "Building some condos over at Nags Head. They want 'em to be ready by summer, when the tourists come pouring in."

I'll give myself credit, I didn't jump up and down and holler hurray. "That's good," I said carefully. "He must get bored just sitting around here. There's not enough to keep him occupied."

"No, I guess not. But it sure kept your grampa busy when he was alive. He could always find aplenty to do."

"That was when we had the farm," I reminded her. "Now it's just the house and yard, and the garden in the summer."

"It's still a lot to do," she said. "More than one person can handle, anyway." She turned off the little light and got up, shoving the sewing bench under the machine with her knee.

I followed her into the kitchen. Her words, spoken without emotion, told more than she realized.

The telephone rang as she passed it and Gramma picked up the receiver. "Yes?" she said loudly. She listened intently, then said, "She's right here. Just a minute."

She thrust it at me like it was a football I should take and run with. "Don't talk too long," she said, turning to the business of making supper.

"Hello?" I said into the mouthpiece, expecting to hear Sue's chatter. Gramma's orders not to talk too long nearly always come when Sue calls.

"Missy, it's Jim."

"Oh. Hi!" How to explain the glad little surge inside me? I strove to sound usual. "Where were you today?"

"So you noticed I wasn't there?"

"Sure I noticed. Anybody as tall as you leaves a large vacancy when they're absent." Was that me talking? What a dumb thing to say!

"I guess you saw Melanie then?"

The scene in the hall came back full force, Melanie's anger, my shock. "Yes, I did."

I waited, but he didn't say anything. He and I have always been efficient and matter-of-fact on the telephone. This silence was dangerous territory.

"We broke up," he said at last.

I was conscious of Gramma with one ear cocked in my direction, figuring out whatever she could from my part of the conversation. "So she told me," I said, "but I didn't get any details."

"Well, what do you think?" he asked.

"What kind of question is that?" I said, feeling more peculiar by the minute.

His laugh sounded self-conscious. "Just joking. Say, can you get away this evening after supper?"

"I've got studying to do," I said. "I almost flunked a physics test today."

"What's that mean—you made an A-minus?"

"No. I really didn't do well."

Gramma threw me a look.

"I have to go help Gramma with supper," I said, clutching the receiver so tightly that my hand ached. "Why'd you call?"

"Just wanted to talk," he said. "Go on and help your gramma. I'll talk to you tomorrow."

It was terrible, how I wanted to keep him on the phone. "You never said where you were today," I said.

"I'll tell you tomorrow," he said, and hung up.

"That boy's been talking to you more in the past two weeks than in the past two years," Gramma observed, as she scrubbed potatoes at the sink.

"He's got girlfriend troubles," I said. "He's been using me for Ann Landers or something."

"Well, I'd be careful about that if I were you," she said. "If something goes wrong, you might get blamed for it."

That was an aspect I hadn't even considered. "What could go wrong?"

Gramma dropped a peeled potato into a pot of cold water with a little bloop. "Whoever she is might think you were out to steal him," she said with a sideways look. "Are you going to set the table or not?"

"Yes, ma'am." I realized I'd just been standing there ever since I hung up the phone. I went over to the cabinet and started taking down plates and glasses and loading them onto a tray to take to the dining room.

I wasn't trying to "steal" Jim. If he and Melanie couldn't get along with each other it sure wasn't *my* fault. I clunked plates and banged silverware, getting madder by the minute. When the tray was empty and the table ready, I marched straight to the phone and dialled Jim's number.

"Hello?" he said.

I lit right in. "I changed my mind. Come over here at eight o'clock. I have some things to say."

"What's wrong?"

"That's what I want to know," I said.

"I don't know if I can come over at eight," he said.

"Well, why not? It was your big idea to start with."

"I know, but . . . Melanie just called and I promised her—"

"Forget it." I hung up, cutting him off in mid-excuse.

Gramma began to hum, a hymn probably, although I couldn't tell for sure. It had a dry little sound like the buzz of an insect and an air of you-better-watch-out about it.

"I set the table," I said, starting out of the kitchen. "I'm going upstairs."

"Somebody's got to make the biscuits," she called after me. "I'm up to my elbows in potatoes."

"I'll be right back!" I hollered, taking the steps two at a time. Truth to tell, I didn't have a reason in the world to go to my room other than to hide my face. I'd barely made it to the top of the stairs when the telephone rang again. I stopped where I was, leaning over the bannister to catch any words. Shortly I heard Gramma's steps padding through the dining room. I moved out of sight, so she wouldn't think I'd been hanging around listening.

"Jim Perkins is on the phone again," she said. "I wish you'd come talk to him. I've got no time to mess with it."

I came back down slowly to give myself time to breathe normally. "Hello," I mumbled into the mouthpiece.

"Why'd you hang up on me? You didn't give me a chance to explain or anything!"

"I'm waiting," I said, looking up at the ceiling and tapping my foot, mostly for Gramma's benefit.

126

"I'll be there as close to eight as I can," he said. "I'll blow the horn."

"All right," I said. This time I hung up more calmly. Avoiding Gramma's eyes, I got the old wooden bread bowl out of the pantry, automatically running my hand along its smooth, curved inside. Grampa had made it for Gramma shortly after they were married.

I got flour, baking powder, buttermilk, and shortening and set to work in a corner of the kitchen out of her way. She hummed "O Happy Day" under her breath as she put the potatoes on and then opened a jar of the green beans we'd put up last summer. I thought about us sitting on the front porch in the evening coolness, snapping beans by the bushel, she and Mama and I, before Uncle Tate came to stay.

"If I was you," she said suddenly, "I'd keep in mind what I was about."

I paused with my hands in the cool squishy dough. "What do you mean, Gramma?"

"If you're planning on leaving here at the end of the summer, you don't want to start up any new attachments."

I bent over the biscuit bowl and shaped and patted the dough into a ball. "No need to worry about *that*," I said. "I already told you."

"I know what you told me."

I floured the breadboard and rolled out the dough, using the old metal cutter that had belonged to Great-Gramma Fields to form large, round biscuits. One by one, I lifted them onto the flat baking pan in neat, nearly-touching rows. Six across, six down. They'd swell in the oven heat and grow together until they looked like a puffy biscuit quilt.

Maybe this is what I really wanted to do: cook in a kitchen that smelled of buttermilk and spices and wait for somebody to come home to me from work. I wouldn't have to move to a new place and live among strangers or try to keep up with students ten times smarter than me. The daydream felt safe and cozy, but letting myself think about it made me feel ashamed.

At 7:55 I waited in the darkened hall by the front door, peering through its glass pane into the night. Sweat filmed my forehead because I'd had my jacket on for fifteen minutes. In the living room, Uncle Tate had moved his chair around just so he could see me where I stood. Mama was in there, too, but she and I couldn't see each other.

"Is he coming in this time?" Uncle Tate asked.

"No, sir." I kept looking out the door.

"Will he ever?"

"Sure—sometime."

"When you get back," Mama said, "maybe you can invite him in for a piece of Ma's cake and some milk."

"I'll ask him," I said. I wouldn't promise.

The mantel clock chimed, making eight holes in the darkness. I stood on one foot, then on the other. I imagined Jim at Melanie's trying to leave. Or maybe she'd gone to *his* house and he couldn't get away without being rude.

I will count to thirty, I thought. If he hasn't come by then, I'll take off my jacket and go upstairs to study.

But of course I didn't. I counted to thirty twice, then three times, more and more slowly. At eight-twenty, I unzipped the jacket and, immediately, as if I'd done a magic trick, two headlights turned into the yard.

"I'm gone," I said tersely, flipping the porch light on, as I opened the door. "I don't know when I'll be back, but it won't be very late."

I closed the door behind me before anybody could respond and hurried down the steps and across the yard. The grass stubble was already covered with frost. I jammed my hands into my pockets to keep them warm and felt the chill seep through my shirtfront from the open jacket.

Jim leaned over and opened the door for me and I climbed in.

"I was about to give up," I said crossly.

"I got here as soon as I could," he said. "That's what I told you I'd do."

"Where are we going?"

"There's not anyplace much where people can have a private conversation," he said, "short of sitting here in the truck and freezing to death."

"We could go to Manteo to the McDonald's," I said. "I'll pay for the gas."

To my surprise, he didn't protest about either driving the twenty-five miles to Manteo or letting me buy the gas. He just drove hard, leaning forward over the steering wheel. Neither of us spoke. The thick stands of trees along either side of the highway and the scarcity of houses made the night seem darker than it was.

I tried several conversation starters in my mind, but

none of them suited. In our growing-up life, Jim and I had had squabbles, but nothing as grim as this. I realized after a few minutes that every muscle in me was on guard. What was I expecting? It was, after all, just Jim and me riding in his pickup toward Manteo.

"What made you change your mind?" he asked suddenly. I'd gotten so used to the silence that I had to think what he meant by the question, had to think what was the honest answer.

"I was ashamed of hanging up on you," I said.

"But before that. When I first call you, you say you have to study. Then in less than fifteen minutes you call *me*, and you sound mad enough to bite, and then you make me feel guilty because meantime I promised Melanie we'd talk. She called after you turned me down. So now both of you are on my case and I'm thinking I ought to quit school and go out to Denver or something!"

Jim's words tumbled about like a catch of fish flopping in the net. I would have laughed, but I've felt the same way and it's not a laughing matter.

"I'm sorry," I said. "It wasn't very considerate of me."

I don't think he expected me to admit I might have been wrong. I doubt if Melanie ever does. To my relief, he leaned back in the seat and eased up on the pedal.

"Well," he said, somewhat grumpily, "what did you want to say?"

I began slowly. "I guess I don't understand about you and Melanie. It's like I'm getting caught in the middle of something without wanting to, and getting blamed for Melanie's problems, and yours."

130

"*I* don't blame you for our problems."

"Well, Melanie does. She thinks I'm her competition or something."

The houses were closer together now. I could see the lights of Manteo against the black sky. The 45-miles-per-hour speed limit sign glowed in the beam of the headlights as we passed. Way up ahead, I saw the McDonald's arch, sticking out from the trees like a yellow neon leg.

"Well, are you?" he asked, so softly that at first I wasn't sure I'd heard him right.

We passed the 35-miles-per-hour sign, and the one that says SPEED CHECKED BY RADAR. Light from houses and stores sprang up, and then the streetlights. He could see my face if he looked.

"I've never meant to be," I said at last. It was the truth as far as it went.

We drove the last little way in silence and turned in at McDonald's. There wasn't much of a crowd. We got out of the truck and went inside. I ordered an apple turnover I didn't want and a Dr. Pepper. Jim ordered a cheeseburger and Coke. We wouldn't look at each other, but I was conscious of his arm within inches of mine as we stood side by side waiting for our order. I paid for mine, like I always do when he and I get something to eat.

"It's something, isn't it?" he said when we were seated. "Kind of a mess, actually."

I suppose he was right, but I didn't like to hear it put in those terms. Neither of us had come right out and said any words that could be used against us, and yet we'd moved to another level and we both knew it. I thought of a book I'd read years ago about a kid hiding in a wardrobe who fell through it into another world. She didn't mean to. She just kept going further and deeper until she tumbled in. Afterward she had trouble finding her way back.

Jim took off his John Deere cap and laid it on the seat beside him. His plaid flannel shirt was rumpled. His face looked worried and exposed. He unwrapped the cheeseburger and took a big bite. Its greasy smell made me feel queasy. I stuck a straw into the Dr. Pepper and sucked up a mouthful of fizz to settle my stomach.

"Why'd you have to go and get that haircut," he said, his mouth half-full. "Why didn't you just stay like you were?"

"I'm no different than I was before!" I snapped. "Nothing's changed about me—not a thing."

He waved one hand to brush that away, to clear the slate for a new start. "I didn't know," he said, "what a difference it'd make. I had no idea."

"I don't know what you're talking about. Please say what you mean."

But judging from the desperation in his eyes, I knew it wouldn't be easy for him, whatever it was.

"It's like I didn't see you until Tuesday. Everything I said Monday about you is true, but it's like . . . it's like I never let myself think about you as . . . as somebody I might—" He gestured feebly, like he was drowning in his own words. Instead of finishing the sentence, he leaped ahead.

"And what I want to know is, why? How could a haircut make so much difference? It makes me think I'm crazy."

"Face it," I said. "Maybe you're like all the guys, just interested in looks. I could be the Airhead of the World, but it'd be okay as long as I looked good."

"No," he said. "Not true."

I didn't feel like arguing. "You and Melanie," I said. "Tell me."

He took another bite of cheeseburger, maybe to delay the telling as long as he could, but I wasn't going anywhere. Finally he swallowed and spoke.

"See, that's what makes me think you . . . it . . . was already working on me and I didn't know it. Monday, when Melanie pulled that trick of showing up, I was so *mad* at her. I couldn't even understand myself how I could be that mad. And after you and I went to the dock and had that long talk, I guess how I felt afterward on the way home was mellowed out." He darted a glance at me to see how I might be taking it. "It was a good feeling. And I thought, well, it's because Missy and I've been pals for so long and we can tell each other what we're really thinking. And I was glad to have a friend like you."

"Yeah," I said. "Me, too."

He brightened at that. But then he remembered what he was supposed to be telling. "So after I dropped you off at the beauty shop, I went home and called Melanie. I tried to explain to her what it was all about—told her the truth. You already know what she said. You guessed it the first time." He sighed, remembering. "And then Tuesday, there you were. Knocked me right off my legs. I

133

couldn't think straight the rest of the day. Or any day since, for that matter."

Nor me, I thought, but I wouldn't say it. I focused my eyes on the unopened turnover.

"Missy, I've broken up with her for good."

"She hates me," I said.

"Not your fault."

"The result's the same as if it was," I answered.

"Look—I know you and me've just been good friends all these years," he said, "but it's different now."

I took the turnover out of the cardboard wrapper and bit into it, thinking how insulted Gramma would be that I'd spent my good money on something so tasteless. I knew if he reached across the table and took my hand, I'd be glad of it. I'd be glad not to have to do end runs around Melanie or some other girl to get to him. I'd be glad of the safeness, of being able to trust him. I'd be glad of the easy way we were around each other.

But there'd be complications, too. Melanie, for one, and the fact that I was getting ready to leave Tucker, doing everything in my power to make my departure come to pass. Gramma's words came back to me from the afternoon's conversation. *You don't want to start up any new attachments.* My face burned. Gramma already knew, even before I did. I'd been counting on matters to stay like they were, with Melanie as Jim's official girlfriend.

"Say something," Jim pleaded. "I feel like a fool." His forearms were propped on the table and now he turned his hands palms up in an I-give-up kind of gesture that did me in.

134

"It's hard," I said, feeling stiff all over. "I'm not used to this."

I thought as I looked at him that I'd never seen a kinder face, except in people much older than we were. If he hadn't been so kind, I would've bolted out the door, maybe run off down the highway on foot toward Tucker.

"I . . . I guess I've had some of the same feelings," I said. "It's why I've been jealous of Melanie. With her around, you and I couldn't be pals anymore. I really missed you, more than I thought I would."

He smiled then, and reached over and squeezed my hand. His is so big that even my huge paw looks reasonably ladylike. My insides did acrobatic tricks I didn't know existed. I squeezed back and watched his face grow serious, even pained.

"We better start back," he said. "I don't want your mom to be mad at me first thing."

First thing. What an odd expression, like we were meeting for the first time. We went out into the night, him with one arm lightly around my waist. I felt as though my feet and legs weren't really mine, and marvelled that I seemed to be walking normally. When we got to the truck, Jim opened the door for me, for the first time in the history of the world. That, more than any other thing, brought home to me what had happened.

Chapter 14

People who've been in car accidents claim they don't remember the actual accident except for glimmers every now and then. They say they have trouble remembering the order of things just before and just afterward. What has happened between Jim and me has the same effect. Every once in a while, I surface and notice faces— Gramma with a kind of purse to her lips, Mama's worry line just above the bridge of her nose, Uncle Tate's gloat. The weird thing is that although I notice the faces, their expressions make no difference to me. I go about in a half-daze, a person morphined.

I sit in class and daydream over pages of history questions or physics problems. The responsible part of me has shrunk to midget size and is tugging frantically at my sleeve yelling *Get your mess together*. The irresponsible part has shot up overnight, moony and lethargic, with practically no conscience at all where school is concerned.

I replay the drive back from Manteo that fateful night, with me sitting as close to Jim as I can and his arm around me. The truck floats. We don't talk much. The intense sweet ache astounds me. I have fallen into another world.

When we drive into the yard, the porch light is on. It seems overly bright. Jim puts the truck in neutral and sets the brake. He does not remove his arm from around me. Then he very calmly turns my face to his and kisses me.

I don't know if I'm breathing or not, but my heart thunders. I can feel it at my neck and in my head. I wonder if anyone has ever had a heart attack while they were kissing. If so, I can certainly understand why.

"You want me to walk you to the door?" Jim asks, his face inches from mine.

I do, but the porch light is too bright. "No—that's okay," I manage to say in a dry whisper. "I'll see you tomorrow at school."

"Yeah." He kisses me one more time, lightly. I slide across the seat and open the door. I am miles from the ground. When my feet finally touch, I am not sure they will hold me up.

But they do. When I reach the door, I turn and wave, although I can barely make out Jim's features through the windshield. I stifle the impulse to blow him a kiss. It doesn't seem like something I'd do.

Everyone has gone to bed. The house's heat smothers without warming me. The smell of fried chicken still lingers in the air and my stomach lurches. I bend down to take off my shoes and see that I am trembling.

It is the first time I understand the word "lovesick."

I turn off the lamp and stand for a few seconds in the darkness until my eyes adjust. Mama has left the nightlight on in the upstairs hall. I can see its dim pink glow from where I stand. Holding my sneakers in my hand, I tiptoe up to my room and a night of exhausting dreams.

Since then, it is like my brain has been divided into two parts. One part gets my body to where it needs to go—to the mailbox to wait for the bus, to classes, to my job at the day-care center, to Sunday school and church, to home and chores. The other part is aflame with happiness. I am hungry but I can't eat.

At school, Sue gives me a funny look. "Wow, Missy— you look terrific!" Her eyes narrow as she studies me, clearly puzzled as to why I should look better than usual. Other than the haircut, which by now everybody's used to, nothing on the outside is different. But when I look in the mirror, I can see it too, something shining through the skin, hidden lights behind my eyes. I catch myself smiling for no good reason.

At school, I always keep my eyes open for Jim, but I try not to show that's what I'm doing. It makes me appear absentminded to others. Sue asks me a question twice before it sinks in.

"I *said* Winston called me last night. He wants to know if you're going to ask him to the dance, because if you're not, he needs to make other plans."

With a huge effort, I look at Sue, trying to remember who Winston is. Then it comes back to me. "Sue, I already told you no. N-O."

Her face falls. "I thought I'd give you one more chance," she says.

And somehow, through my new powers, I can see that she has a huge crush on Winston. She is trying to find a way for him to be here, even if it means he has to date another girl.

"Why're you looking at me like that?" she says.

"I was just trying to think who else you could get to ask him," I say. "What about Kristi or maybe Beth?"

Her head is already shaking before I get the names out of my mouth. I can see why. No doubt she thinks she would have better control over things if I am Winston's date.

"Well," I say, walking away from her, "I hope you find somebody."

I head for my locker, not because I need to get anything but because it is my base, my permanent school address. The bell will ring any minute and I'll have to sprint to make it to class, but I won't have to talk to Sue once Mr. Preston's rules go into effect.

And there is Jim hovering near my locker, eyeing it as though he wonders if I've shut myself in there. I am still not used to the surge of happiness I feel at the sight of him. I think maybe I'm giving off rads.

"Hi!" I say.

He turns toward the sound of my voice, his face alight, too. The bell rings. It is the ugliest noise I've ever heard.

"I've been waiting for you," he says, putting a tentative hand on my arm.

"Sorry. Sue waylaid me. She's been trying to get me to ask some friend of hers to the JanDance."

"You better say no," he tells me. "You're going with me."

I smile, relieved that he's said it out loud. "I'm going to be late. I've got to run."

"Will I see you at lunch?"

"Sure. Back table." And I tear off down the hall running, which is forbidden. For once I'm not caught and I fall into my seat gasping. Mr. Preston slams the door as soon as I'm inside the room and gives me a questioning look. I don't even blush.

Only years of discipline and habit get me through the morning of exam review. I am living for lunch, no matter that I won't be able to eat any of it.

I skip the carton of milk so as not to waste any time standing in line to pay for it. I take my sandwich and apple straight to the back of the cafeteria where I know Jim will be waiting for me.

I'm not prepared to see him and Melanie deep in conversation, just like all the other lunchtimes this year. I stop suddenly and somebody runs into me.

"Sorry," I mumble.

"You oughtta give signals," they say, but I don't even look to see who it is.

I'm astonished at my own jealous outrage—I didn't know I had it in me. Part of me wants to go off in a corner and sulk until Jim notices and comes to find me. But another part of me is more adventurous. I head for the table without dwelling on the consequences.

Jim looks up first. His expression turns despairing. Melanie, seeing the change in him, turns to face me.

I think: *Fight! Fight!* Because it feels like those big hall or playground squabbles between two people that end up in the middle of a ring of spectators. I have always stayed as far away from them as I could, but now I can see that circumstances might put a person in the middle whether they want to be there or not.

"Hello," I say. I sit down across from them and take great care in opening my sandwich bag. I don't look directly at either of them, but I can sense Melanie's head swivelling toward Jim again. Maybe she wants him to run me off.

"Well!" Melanie says in a huff of air that I think I can feel all the way across the table. "If you don't mind, we're having a private conversation."

"I don't mind," I say, taking a bite of sandwich. I hope I will be able to swallow without throwing up.

"Come on, Jim," she says. "Let's move."

I still don't look at them. I chew and chew.

"I don't think so," Jim says in a voice so strained I don't think I'd recognize it if he wasn't right across from me. "I told Missy I'd meet her here for lunch."

The longest silence follows his words. All the noise in the cafeteria cannot overcome it.

"I'm not leaving until we're through with our conversation," Melanie says at last, her voice low and intense like a sports announcer's right next to a microphone. "And we're not having that conversation in front of *her!*"

The pronoun snakes out at me like a curse. I swallow the bread and peanut butter before it's ready to go down.

With nothing to drink at hand, I think maybe I have just committed suicide.

"Excuse me a minute," I say in mid-strangle, getting up. "I have to get some milk."

It doesn't really matter at this point whether Melanie thinks she's won or not. I plan to come back as soon as I make my purchase.

A full five minutes passes before I can get the carton of milk, open it, and send the bolus of peanut butter and bread on down to where it belongs. By the time I get back to the table Melanie is gone and Jim is the picture of misery.

"Are you all right?" he asks.

I nod. "I could ask you the same thing."

"Lord, I've never been in a mess like this in my life!" he breathes, rubbing the top of his head. "Melanie says she's changed her mind."

"About what?"

"About us breaking up. She doesn't want to."

I stop chewing and look at him hard. I feel a twinge of fear. Can she do that?

"I told her it's no use," he says. "I asked her had she forgotten how much we fought and squabbled, but it's like she doesn't remember that part . . . or doesn't want to."

I am so relieved I take a deep breath. "Well," I say, feeling generous, "I don't mind you talking to Melanie to straighten it all out, if that's what it takes."

As soon as I say the words, I am astounded. Already I am regarding him as my personal possession, the very thing I have hated so about Melanie.

"Forget I said that," I mutter, embarrassed. "It's not really any of my business. That's between you and Melanie."

"Yeah," he answers, looking at me curiously.

But Melanie haunts me. I can feel her at my elbow, across a room, in the crowded hall, on the schoolground. Actually I only catch glimpses of her every now and then. Still, I live in dread that I will round a corner and meet her face to face. I wonder if she ever felt that way about me.

Although Jim and I see each other when we can, after school or at night, we manage to keep our cover of friendship at school. He hasn't said so, but I'm pretty sure he hasn't told Melanie about us. At home, I have not made any open announcements, but I have decided to tell the truth if anybody asks. So far, no one has, and nothing seems to lead into my saying, "Well, Jim and Melanie broke up and now it's Jim and me."

Most peculiar of all is the fact that nobody in my family comments when I drop everything at 8:00 to go out for a hamburger with Jim on a school night. I convince myself that they are convinced at last that we really are just friends. The irony is not lost on me.

Exam week I ask him over to study on Tuesday night. I hold off until supper to announce that he is coming. I have practiced upstairs saying it in an offhand manner. After the blessing, during the passing of food, I say, "Oh, by the way—Jim's coming over tonight to study."

"Fine!" Gramma and Mama say quickly, at one and the same time.

My heart sinks. I see right away that I haven't fooled anybody.

"You can study here on the dining-room table," Mama goes on, smiling too brightly.

"Thank you," I say.

"It's about time he came over," is all Uncle Tate says. His tone is so mild I become instantly wary. I steel myself for a snide remark, but it doesn't come.

"You still being Ann Landers?" Gramma asks, setting the biscuit basket in front of me.

I can feel heat in my cheeks. "No, ma'am." I take a biscuit and split it with my knife. The steam rises from its center, moist and buttermilky, but my stomach is in such a knot the smell isn't even appetizing.

After dessert, Uncle Tate excuses himself from the table, but he doesn't go directly to the living room and turn on the television as is his custom. Instead he walks over to the window and with the side of his hand wipes a little peephole in the condensed moisture on the pane. He puts his eye close to the window and peers out into the night, his hands in his pockets, his shoulders slumping.

What is he looking for? I wonder, struck by this curious behavior. Mama studies him with her head to one side. Gramma offers him a second piece of pie. More food is her way of getting a person's mind off their troubles. Lately, I haven't thought of Uncle Tate as having troubles, only as *causing* them.

He turns suddenly from the window. "What time is Jim coming?" he asks.

"Around eight," I say. I want to add that I hope Uncle

Tate will be polite and not make embarrassing remarks, but I know better than to put ideas in his head.

Uncle Tate looks at the kitchen clock. "I got a couple of errands to run," he mumbles. He leaves the dining room to fetch his coat.

We three look at each other with raised eyebrows. In all the time Uncle Tate has been here, he has never once gone out after supper, except to Wednesday night prayer meetings and Sunday evening worship at Foursquare.

He returns with his coat already zipped to the neck and his khaki hunting cap low on his head. He looks more than ever like a squash.

"I don't know what time I'll be back," he says, almost daring us by his tone to ask him where he's going. But we don't. There seems to be a silent agreement among us to show him how it's done.

"You don't need to leave the door unlocked," he says on the way out. "I've got a key."

"Well," Gramma says abruptly, pushing herself up from the table, "we better get these dishes cleared and washed before your company comes."

Mama and I rise, too, and begin the automatic dance we know so well, passing in and out between kitchen and dining room without bumping, each knowing her part. We don't speak of Uncle Tate, but I imagine him driving deeper and deeper into the darkness, going farther and farther away. No matter how hard I try, I cannot imagine his destination.

Chapter 15

When I finally put down my pencil and flexed my fingers at the end of the physics exam on Friday afternoon, I felt like a grain sack hanging on a nail, empty and shapeless. Everyone else in the class was still writing when I took my paper up to Mr. Francis's desk. He nodded and actually smiled.

Free at last! I felt as light as a human on the moon, but not even a senior finished with exams can wander the halls without permission or purpose. Without really thinking what I was doing, I went downstairs to Ms. Hollins's office. I tapped lightly on the door. Maybe she wouldn't be in and I could wait another day to—

"Come in!"

I pushed the door open.

"Well, Missy! I'm glad you came by—I've hardly seen your face this week. All finished?"

"About fifteen minutes ago," I said. "My head's so empty it echoes."

She laughed and pointed to the seat next to her desk. "Come catch me up, then."

Suddenly shy, I ducked my head. "Well, things are . . . sort of different since I talked to you last."

Ms. Hollins's right eyebrow went up. "How so?"

I took a deep breath and began, not knowing how much I'd tell. Once I started, I couldn't seem to stop. All the time, I watched her eyes. The more I talked, the more serious they became.

"Well," she said softly when I'd finished, "things happen in a hurry, don't they? It sounds as though this thing with Jim kind of sneaked up on both of you."

"Yes," I said.

"How does it affect your plans?" she asked.

"What do you mean?"

"Next year. College."

"My plans are the same," I said, sitting straighter.

"That's good." She nodded. "I know you have those interviews coming up soon at Moriah."

"I don't like to think about them," I confessed. "I'll probably do something super stupid."

"Let me tell you something, Missy." She leaned toward me, resting an arm on the desk. "I don't suppose there's any way you could know what an exceptional person you are, other than somebody telling you. So I'm telling you. I've been a few places. I know what I'm talking about. You have a good chance, believe me."

I wanted to believe her. At least, I thought I did. If she

was right, I could be a student at Moriah College next year this time with no financial worries. It was what I'd hoped for and worked toward all these years.

"Well, I sure hope you're right!" I stood up to go. My smile felt like a mask I was holding in front of my real face, and when I left her office I didn't feel so light anymore.

In the upstairs hall, I met Sue just coming out of Mr. Francis's classroom.

"God, that was a hard exam!" she raved. "My hand is permanently cramped. How'd you get through so quick?"

"Two hours is not quick," I said.

"You want a ride home?" She rushed past me toward her locker. "I'm leaving now."

I followed her out to the red Honda, listening with half an ear as she chattered on about everything that came to mind. She skipped from the exam to what she was going to wear to the JanDance to . . . inevitably . . . Winston. I sighed inwardly.

"He was *so* disappointed you didn't ask him," she told me as we got in the car.

I buckled the seat belt and wondered whether I should tell her that I knew her secret. "He'll get over it," I said instead.

"And there's no *reason* for it," she went on, starting the engine and zipping out of the lot. "I mean, here you are going to the dance by yourself—a perfectly good invitation gone to waste."

"Sue, it's too late now. Why're we talking about this?"

148

"Not really," she said. "He could still get here if you wanted him."

I laughed. "Have you forgotten? A person from another school has to be approved."

She flashed me a guilty, sidelong look. "Well, actually, I took care of that. I mean, I didn't *know* if you might change your mind at the last minute, so I went ahead and put him on the list."

I sat straight up. "As *my* date?"

She nodded, shrinking a little at my bellow. "But of course it doesn't really matter now, does it?"

"Yes it does!" I hollered. "It matters a *lot*. I *have* a date. I've actually been *asked* by someone, although I know that's hard for you to take in. I told you at least three times *no!* What are you, stupid or something?"

She kept both hands on the steering wheel and drove, her eyes wide. "Wh . . . why didn't you tell me?" she said at last, in a subdued voice.

"Have I got to tell you everything? Besides, you never listen. I told you I didn't want a date with Winston, but I might as well have been talking to the moon!" I folded my arms across my chest and glared out of the window on my side, gritting my teeth to keep from saying other insulting things that came to mind.

After a time, I became aware of the unusual silence, especially the fact that she hadn't even asked who I was going with. I turned my head to see her biting her lower lip. Tears tracked down her freckled cheeks.

"*Now* what?" I said gruffly.

"I didn't mean to make you mad." She sniffed and wiped her face with her hand.

"Well, put yourself in my place," I said. "How would you feel if somebody was trying to run your life whether you wanted them to or not?"

She shrugged. "Mom does—a lot. I've sort of gotten used to it."

"Well, I'm not used to it," I said, "but I'm sorry I yelled at you."

She gave me a shaky smile. "It's okay. I guess I deserved it."

"Tell me the truth," I said. "Are you expecting Winston to show up tonight?"

Tears welled up again. She nodded. "It was the only way I could think of to get him into the dance. I can't stand it that I've got to go with Barry instead."

"Why not break the date with Barry?"

"That wouldn't be nice, Missy."

Somehow I could hear Sue's mom saying those words. Mrs. Gibbs puts a great premium on being nice.

"Well, knowing how you feel about Winston, I'm sure glad I *don't* have a date with him," I said. "I'd be left sitting in a corner alone most of the night."

She had enough conscience to look ashamed. "Yeah. It was a dumb idea."

This was the first time I could ever remember seeing Sue really glum. I felt sorry for her.

"I guess I'll call him when I get home and tell him not to come," she went on. Wrapped up as she was in her own problem, she was about to drive past our house.

"Better slow down—the driveway is right there," I warned.

The tires squealed as she stomped the brake and veered into the yard, digging a couple of ruts in the soft wet dirt. I opened the door and got out.

"You haven't told me who you're going with," she said.

The question was long overdue, but I guess by that time, I thought she wasn't going to ask.

"Jim," I said, and slammed the door so I couldn't hear anything else she might say. "Thanks for the ride."

Not to be outfoxed, she opened the door on her side and leaned out. "Didn't he and Melanie just break up?"

I nodded. I began moving toward the house, waving, to let her know the conversation was over, as far as I was concerned.

"He's on the rebound!" she yelled. "You have to watch out for guys on the rebound—they get mixed up about who you are!"

I made it to the front porch and got the door open. "See you tonight!" I called, and then shut it quickly behind me.

That night, I wore the new plaid skirt and Mama's oversized green sweater, which is not oversized on me. She helped me fix my hair so it would look like I just walked out of AyDee's.

She laid the brush on the dresser, hesitating a moment as though there was something else she wanted to say. I could've asked *What is it?* But I didn't. "See you downstairs," she said as she went out.

"Thanks," I called after her, but she must not have heard me.

I thought about her at my age, never going out with

anyone. Even if she had, I'm sure Grampa and Gramma would've handed out a long list of cautions to keep her from having fun.

I liked having Jim knock on the door to be let in by Mama. I liked coming downstairs and seeing his glad face when he looked at me. I liked Uncle Tate's strained politeness as he and Jim shook hands in the way that men do, as though they're meeting each other for the first time. I liked Gramma's asking about Jim's folks. The whole scene was like a 1950s dream date or something, right down to Jim's helping me with my jacket and our leaving with Mama's "Have a good time!" hanging in the air at our backs.

We had a good laugh about going all dressed up to the dance in the fishy-smelling truck.

"The *least* you could've done for the occasion would've been to pile the tools in the back," I teased.

"I was afraid it'd send you into shock," he said. "Spoil the whole evening."

I leaned back, laughing, happy. At that point, I would have laughed at anything anyone said. "So how'd you do on your English exam today?" I asked him.

"I don't know. All right, I guess."

"Physics was awful," I said, "but I finished it in two hours. I sure am glad I studied chapter eight last night or—"

"Look, could we just not talk about exams and school for one night?" he interrupted. "Exams are *over*. Tonight we're having fun."

Startled by the heat behind the words, I could only mumble, "Sorry. Just a bad habit of mine."

In the short uncomfortable silence, he reached over and put his hand on the back of my neck under my hair. "Don't worry. I'll try to break you of it." He smiled, then added, "Who'd've ever thought it? You and me together, I mean?"

"Not me," I said. "It was the last thing on my mind."

"How about now?" he asked.

I had to think for a couple of seconds what he meant. "Now it's *not* the last thing on my mind."

"Is it the first?"

"What is this?" I laughed and poked him in the ribs. "Are you feeling insecure or something?"

"Maybe," he answered.

I got a kind of tight feeling inside.

"What's the matter?" he asked.

"Nothing. I was just thinking."

He sighed. "You do a lot of that, don't you?" He removed his hand from my neck to turn on the radio. The Judds were belting out "Girls' Night Out." He turned up the volume and sang along with them.

"What's wrong with thinking?" I raised my voice to be heard over the music.

"Nothing!" He turned up the sound another notch. I rolled down the window to let some of it escape, but the cold wind rushing in was too much for me. In a minute, I closed the window and joined the singing in self-defense. We and the Judds sang all the way to the school.

Since the parking lots close to the buildings were already full, Jim parked the truck at the day-care center. We walked from there across the highway to the gym. Strains of music leaked through its walls, blasting loudly when someone opened a door to enter or leave. I liked having Jim's arm at my back, but I could also feel the beginnings of self-consciousness. We'd kept cool up to now, but after tonight, we'd be an item. We'd be teased. We'd be paired. The "Vacuum Cleaner" column in the school newspaper would mention us by our initials and make sly remarks.

Some girls would rejoice or take comfort in that, but not me. My steps slowed.

"What's the matter?" Jim asked.

"Nothing," I said. "Just something in my shoe."

It wasn't a complete lie, if you consider cold feet something.

Twists of blue and white crepe paper dripped from the gym's steel rafters. In a far corner, among a jumble of speakers and other sound equipment, Chuck Bishop played deejay with tapes and albums students had donated for the dance. In the opposite corner, Ms. Hollins and Mr. Preston presided over a long table full of food and drink. The bleachers along one wall had been pushed back to make more room for dancing. Those along the opposite wall collected coats and nondancers.

"Are we gonna stand here all night or what?" Jim said close to my ear. "I'm ready to dance."

The music from Chuck's amplifiers had become slow and dreamy. I began taking off my coat. Immediately Jim was helping me, letting his hands linger on my shoulders. When he took my hand and led me out onto the dance floor, I gave up trying to fool anybody. Jim pulled me close to him as though we'd been dancing forever. My head fitted under his chin, my ear rested against his chest.

I listened to the music and to his heartbeat and blanked out everything else. My usually stumbling feet seemed to know what to do.

"You're mighty quiet," he said. "Thinking again?"

I pulled away slightly to look at him. "Actually, I was just listening to the music. My brain is so fried after all the cramming I've done, I'm glad I don't have to think."

"Yeah. I know what you mean. I only have one more round of exams in the spring and I'm done with them for life. I can't wait!" He grinned down at me. "Sure you don't want to change your mind about going to college?"

"Ha!" Again I felt the tightness inside. I leaned against his chest again. "We're not talking about school and such tonight—remember?"

When the music came to an end, he held me a second longer than the last note, then led me off the dance floor. Quite suddenly, out of the corner of my eye, I caught a glimpse of Melanie in a hot pink sweater, but I looked away quickly. I wondered if Jim had seen her.

At the refreshment table, Ms. Hollins kept a cool face as she poured our punch and made small talk. At some point, Sue appeared at my side, with Barry looming behind her in all his football-player thickness.

"Having fun, Missy?" In spite of the fact that she'd only learned this afternoon that Jim was my date, she had a way of looking as though she knew everything about us.

"Yes," I said, stiff-lipped. "I hope *you* are." I intended my words to be weighted. If she so much as hinted at making pointed remarks, I would bring up the name Winston. She must have caught my drift.

"Oh, sure!" She smiled with a fierce purposefulness. Barry's beefy hands rested possessively on her shoulders.

"Hey!" Jim touched my elbow. "Hurry up with the punch so we can dance."

"I'm not so good at fast dancing," I warned him.

"Don't worry about it!" He took the paper cup from me and set it on the table, then whirled us out into the music, a skydiver leaping into a cloud. I flung myself about, self-consciously imitating his moves.

"Don't be so stiff," he panted as we rocked face to face. "Just let go and listen to the music!"

Nothing makes me freeze up like somebody telling me I'm stiff. Discouraged and sweaty, I glanced around. Three couples away, I saw Melanie and her date. He, like me, was doing the best he could, but he wasn't even in her league. She danced with abandon, eyes closed and head thrown back, like her survival depended on it. Maybe it did.

Jim and Melanie should be dancing together.

The thought came to me so clearly I could hear it. With a major effort, I pushed it down and buried it.

Time flew by. We danced, talked, danced some more. When the last dance ended, I had wound down to a kind of half-stupefied state of contentment. What a difference in tonight and how I'd felt at Sue's party two weeks ago! The self-consciousness about us from the beginning of the evening was gone for good. I couldn't stop smiling. This was *happy*.

We moved toward the exit in a clump of bodies, which I didn't mind because it gave Jim an excuse to have his arm around me. We were practically upon Melanie before

I saw her standing just inside the door in her quilted coat. Her reproachful eyes focused on Jim. There was no sign of her dancing buddy. Maybe she'd sent him home.

"Hello, Jim," she said, ignoring me.

"Hi," he answered. Then like a fool he added, "J'have fun?"

"What do *you* think?"

"Sorry," he said, ducking his head a little.

"I'll bet!" she said heavily, looking past him at me.

We walked in silence across the highway. It took a lot of self-control not to look over my shoulder to see whether Melanie was following us. I had this vision of her climbing into the truck to spy on us, or to lie in wait for Jim after he dropped me off at home.

"Sorry about that," he mumbled as he opened the door for me to get in. "Melanie's taking this thing harder than I thought she would."

"It's okay," I said. "Not your fault."

But I couldn't work up any anger toward Melanie. The radio blared on as soon as Jim turned the key in the ignition. I reached over and turned it off.

"I want to know about you and her," I said. "How you got together."

I think he was surprised I came right out and asked, maybe as surprised as I was to be asking. He put the truck in gear, turned on the heater, the blower, the lights. I wondered if he'd heard me. He backed the truck out of the parking space, moved to the edge of the highway to find an opening in the line of leaving vehicles. I was about to ask again, when he finally spoke.

"I found out Melanie liked me. You know how it is—

some girl'll come up to you and say 'I have a friend thinks you're really cute,' and all that junk. So then I started noticing her. One thing led to another. We started going out." He lowered his head, like a person ashamed. "I wasn't dating anybody else. It seemed like an okay thing to do."

"I thought you really liked her," I said.

"Well. I *did*. I mean, I admit she turned me on." He shot a look at me when he said that, to see how I'd take it. I wouldn't give him any satisfaction. I kept my face plain and thanked my stars for the dark. "And I guess I was flattered by the attention," he went on. "Girls don't exactly fall all over themselves on my account."

"So what went wrong?"

"Oh, just a combination of things," he said vaguely.

"Such as?"

"She started hinting around about getting married, having kids. I'm not ready for that."

"What else?"

"You."

"What?"

"That's what it comes down to. Not that I *knew*." A break in the stream of cars allowed him to get out onto the highway. I kept hearing *You, You, You*, as though he'd said it into a deep well.

"You came up with this stuff about why didn't anybody ask you out," he said. "I found out I didn't want anybody else to ask you out, and I had to face up to why."

We were almost to my house by now. The dashboard clock said 12:20, ten minutes till curfew, not enough time for such weighty matters.

158

"Missy, with you and me, it's chemistry and more. Going with Melanie I was missing you the whole time, but pushing it down, telling myself you'd always be around."

We reached the mailbox and he turned into the yard, stopping the truck outside the pool of light from the porch. He turned off the engine and the lights, then turned and faced me fully.

The air inside the truck cooled. I imagined Mama lying in her bed upstairs, her ears open to this silence in the yard below. I had a sad feeling, a sense of time wasted. I'd done my share of pretending, too. I moved closer to him and leaned my head on his shoulder. He put his arms around me and cuddled me, kissing my face and hair.

"It's going on February, Jim," I said bleakly. "I wish . . . we'd known before."

Chapter 16

The Saturday morning after the dance I slept until ten, which in Gramma's view is sinful, but she didn't say a word about it when I finally wandered downstairs. Uncle Tate and Mama had both gone to work. Gramma had long since tidied the kitchen and was at the sewing machine, this time making a bedspread to match the curtains in my room.

"You shouldn't go to the trouble, Gramma. I'm not going to be around that much longer." The lump that came up in my throat when I spoke surprised and unnerved me. I turned away so she wouldn't see my face.

"You do plan to come home once in a while, don't you?" she asked. "Far as I know, we don't plan to pack away every reminder of you once you're gone."

I tried to laugh, but I couldn't make it happen. She got

up from the sewing machine and followed me into the kitchen.

"I'll fix you some eggs."

I protested. "I can fix my own breakfast, Gramma."

"Sit down," she ordered.

I did, not having the energy to argue. I leaned my elbows on the table and propped my head in my hands while she puttered about frying sausage, scrambling eggs, brewing coffee, messing up her kitchen again for my sake. After a while, she said, "You must not've had a very good time last night."

"But I *did*. About the best time I've had since I was a kid."

She stopped to look at me. "Then how come you look and sound like a hound that's been left out in the rain?"

"I'm just not used to staying out so late."

But Gramma wasn't fooled. She put my breakfast on a plate and brought it over to the table. "Move your elbows."

I obeyed, leaning my head over the hot food to breathe deeply. "Thanks, Gramma. That smells delicious."

She dismissed the thanks and the compliment with a wave of her hand as she pulled out a chair and sat opposite me. "What's the matter?"

I tried to joke. "My life's gotten complicated all of a sudden, that's all."

Her eyes continued to bore into me and I felt the truth rising to the top. The next thing I knew, it was coming out of my mouth. "Gramma, it's Jim. I've found out I really love him. And he loves me."

"I thought it must be something like that." She clucked and sighed impatiently. "You been going around all moony-eyed for days, now."

I made some feeble protest but she ignored it.

"You managed to get through most of your high school years without getting mixed up with some boy," she said. "How come it had to happen now?"

"It's nothing I set out to do."

"Hah! Why'd you get your hair cut, then? Wasn't a thing the matter with it the way it was."

I was silent. How could I explain I had hoped the changed appearance might get me some dates, a social life, so I wouldn't be vulnerable to love like Mama had been?

"Do you think Jim's your last chance?" Gramma asked. "Do you think no other male will ever give you the time of day?"

"It's not like that, Gramma." I struggled to stay calm, to keep from yelling at her. "I wouldn't've picked Jim if it'd been left up to cool-headed sanity. It makes no sense at all, but it happened. I can't help my feelings."

"That's not the point," she said. "It's what you *do* with them. Look at your mama. When she wasn't much older than you she let her feelings take over her life, and it ruined everything she'd worked for."

Yes, I thought, but maybe it was because she'd never been allowed her feelings. The difference in Mama's life and mine, so far as I could see, was that I had her for a mother instead of somebody like Gramma. But I couldn't say that.

"How old were you and Grampa when you got married?" I asked. "How did you know it was the real thing?"

My question caught her by surprise, pushed her backward into memory when she didn't expect it. I saw in her eyes the quick softness that thinking of Grampa always put there.

"I was twenty, he was twenty-two. We'd known each other all our lives. There just came a time we knew."

"Jim and I have been best friends since before kindergarten," I said.

She frowned a little, considering the point. Then her face cleared.

"Your grampa and I wanted the same things," she said. "He'd bought this land. He wanted to fix up the house and have children and farm. I wanted to be a wife and mother, a helpmeet, as it says in the Bible. I didn't have funny notions about going off somewhere else or having an outside job."

She looked me straight in the eye. "In the case of you and Jim—who's going to follow who? Is he planning to go to school somewhere like you are?"

I shook my head. She'd cut straight to the heart of the problem. "But the other possibility," I said carefully, "is that . . . maybe . . . I won't go off to school."

"Hmph! Hold yourself back so you'd make a closer match?" She didn't try to hide her scorn.

"But I might go to college and then find out that here's where I want to be after all, with Jim." I was hardly able to keep from wailing. "And in the meantime he might give up on me, find somebody else."

"It's a chance you have to take, isn't it?" she told me. "A person can't have everything they want in life."

I wanted to say *Why not?* But I knew better.

"What would you do if you were me?" I asked her.

"Oh, no, you don't!" She leaned back. "You're not going to catch me like that. You're the one has to decide."

"I thought you didn't much like the idea of my going off to college."

"You're not going to use what I think as an excuse to stay home," she told me, thumping the tabletop with one bent finger. "You never paid attention to me before, so don't use me as an excuse now. I just hope we've raised up a girl with good common sense."

Early in the afternoon, I rode my bike to Cedar Bay. It was a sunny day, but cold and windy. The waves crested with whitecaps as far as I could see, beyond the mouth of the bay and out into the Sound. The chill made my eyes water.

I left the bike leaning against a tree and walked down the slight slope of land to the main pier. Mr. Perkins's boat *The Marbeth* was in its usual place, meaning that neither he nor Jim was here. I waved to the fishermen I knew and walked on out, all the way to the end of the pier, not stopping until the toes of my shoes projected beyond the last plank. Plenty of times before now, I've wished I could keep on walking out onto the water, taking a path to parts of the world I've only heard about but never seen.

But not now.

I sat down on the splintery boards and let my legs hang

164

over the side. The waves splashed against the pilings, spraying upward in droplets that landed on my shoes.

What was I supposed to do?

I called up the face of every person I cared about who cared about me and what I did. Mama first, of course. Her hopes had been on the rise ever since the day I came home with that Financial Aid Form. If I told her now I was having second thoughts, what would she think of me? She'd love me regardless of the choice I made, but she'd be disappointed.

I moved on to Ms. Hollins and cringed a little inside. She wouldn't take my second thoughts lying down, especially after all she'd done to get me this far. Mr. Preston had been cheering me on for years. Would he be surprised if I backed out, or would he just sigh and say he was afraid all along that's what I'd do? The thought didn't make me feel any better.

Mr. Francis had said it discouraged him to be in the export business, and yet I knew he wouldn't be happy to learn he wasn't exporting me after all. Mrs. Arnot would lecture me and tell me not to make up my mind yet. Ironically, Uncle Tate might be the only person, other than Jim, who would support my staying here.

I felt the pier vibrating under me, as though from someone's footsteps. When I turned, I saw Jim sprinting toward me, waving as he ran.

"How'd you know I was here?" I shouted against the wind.

"I called your house. Your Gramma told me you were heading this way. Thought I'd find out for myself."

He lowered himself to sit beside me. Then he wrapped me in his arms and kissed me long and hard enough to wipe out everything on my mind.

"Hey—whoa!" I said when I came up for air. "I'm here to think."

"Wouldn't you know it?" He rolled his eyes toward the sky and shook his head in mock despair, but he wouldn't let go of me. Instead he pulled me closer and added, "If you *have* to think, I hope it's about me."

"In a way it was." I laughed.

"Well, y'know you don't have to do that. You can just call me up and I'll be here in the flesh."

I poked him in the stomach, still laughing, already feeling lighter. He laughed, too, but then he got serious and looked me in the eye.

"Last night was great," he said.

I nodded. "Yeah, it was, wasn't it?"

"I mean, none of the stuff you usually worry about on a date, like how you look or what you say or . . . or whether the other person's having a good time. *You* know."

"Well, I'm not exactly what you'd call the most socially experienced person in the world," I said. "I don't have anything to compare it to like *you* do."

He made a face at me, excusing the dig. "So what were you thinking about?"

I focused on the farthest point I could see, the faint horizon line almost lost in haze. But I felt him next to me, solid and warm.

"Jim, do you want me to go away in the fall?"

166

"Now that's a funny question! It's what you've always planned to do, isn't it? All I've ever heard out of you for years is you're going to college come hell or high water." He seemed angry that I'd asked. "I can't imagine you doing anything else."

"Like you being a fisherman?"

"Well, y- yes, I suppose."

I didn't miss the hesitation. "What's the difference?"

"Maybe none," he allowed, "but at least fishing's what I grew up with, what my dad does, what *I* do. I love it. It's not . . . *hard*."

I saw what he was getting at. My going to college had been a struggle for money, for approval, for family support, for the knowledge I'd need to qualify. None of it had been easy.

"Do you think that's a sign it's wrong?" I asked him. "Its being hard?"

"No, not necessarily. But I'm sure glad I don't have to knock myself out like you have."

And why did I have to?

Except for Mama, none of my family had ever made any effort to get away from here. It was in their blood to stay in Tucker and do whatever came to hand, or so it seemed. Bill Cord came unbidden to my mind.

When two people make a baby, they don't think much about what it means down the line, especially when one of them isn't around to influence the outcome. Maybe a few rebel chromosomes were sticking pins in me. Much as I denied Bill Cord's genes, maybe that's where this drive had come from.

"It's not fair!" I shouted, struggling to my feet. I moved to the railing and gripped it with my mittened hands.

I felt Jim beside me and looked up into his face. I saw what I was feeling reflected in his eyes and in the set of his jaw. I wasn't the only one with a war going on inside. Ashamed, I grabbed him around the waist and hugged him tight, burying my face in his leather jacket. In a moment, his arms tightened around me. The wind roared past us. The sun danced on the water. I closed my eyes against the future.

"If you said you didn't want me to go away, I wouldn't," I said, my words muffled against his chest.

"You think I'm crazy?" His voice cracked on the word. "I can't do that. You know I can't."

For a couple of seconds, I considered picking a fight with him. I imagined myself saying, *You don't really love me, do you?* Or something to that effect. But we don't play games like that with each other.

"I'm supposed to go to Moriah next weekend for interviews," I reminded him. "For the big scholarship. I'm . . . not sure anymore that it's what I want to do."

He was silent. Through the cracks between the planks, I could see the water moving in biased waves toward the sloping land.

"I don't think it's right," I went on, "to go through the motions when my heart's not in it. I'd just be stringing people along."

"Ms. Hollins would say you ought to do it for the experience," he said.

"They *all* would. They'd be counting on the experience to change my mind."

"What's the matter then—you afraid they might be right?"

"Whose side are you on, anyway?" I asked crossly, taking a step back.

"I'm trying real hard not to be on any side," he said gently, "and it's not easy. You gotta do what you gotta do."

"Some friend *you* are," I said, half-joking, half-mournful. I linked my arm in his and we started walking back toward the shore.

"But you don't have to look so down," he added. "This is today. I'll take you to a movie in Manteo tonight if you can quit feeling sorry for yourself long enough to go."

"You!" I balled up my fists and pummelled him on the back until he ran. I chased him all the way back to the truck, laughing and crying at the same time.

Chapter 17

Uncle Tate, Mama, Gramma, and I sat around the kitchen table having Sunday breakfast. Uncle Tate was dressed for church, minus his coat and tie. His suspenders dug into his shirt at the shoulder, puffing the sleeves slightly. He leaned forward over the table to slurp his coffee from a too-full cup. Watching him made me think about Grampa, who was a much bigger man than Uncle Tate. But Uncle Tate had outdone Grampa in one respect, and that was in showing off his religion.

As the thought passed through my mind, I suddenly realized that Uncle Tate had cut back on his scripture quoting. In fact, I couldn't recall his doing it in the past several days.

"What're you staring at?" he asked me, setting the coffee cup in its saucer and sitting straight up. "Have I got butter on my chin or something?"

"N . . . no," I stammered. "I didn't know I was staring."

"Well, you were. You were looking at me like I'd grown another head!"

I began to invent. "I think I was just sort of staring into space. You know, not really seeing what I was looking at."

"Daydreaming," Gramma said, giving me a knowing look.

"I was thinking about Grampa," I said, which was true enough. "I miss how we all used to go to church together when he and Aunt Mary were still here." I hoped to turn the conversation in a more comfortable direction, away from me and my daydreams.

Uncle Tate lifted his cup for another slurp. "Well," he said with just a tad of righteousness in his tone, "I invited y'all to come to Foursquare anytime you wanted to."

"Yes, you did," said Gramma, "and I've decided I just might go with you this morning, Tate."

He choked and spluttered. Droplets of coffee spattered on the table and on his shirtfront. The cup clattered into the saucer. He wheezed, coughed, turned red, submitted to a pounding on the back by Mama and a glass of water from me. Finally, in a weak voice, he said, "Well, actually, this might not be such a good day for you to do that, Ma. How about next Sunday?"

Gramma looked stunned. The last thing she or any of us expected was a turndown. "Why isn't it a good day?"

"Well, I . . . uh . . . won't be coming straight home after the services," he said. His already ruddy complexion turned darker.

Gramma's eyes pierced him. For an instant, I saw her

as the mama she used to be, and him as the little boy.

"I *see*," she said.

But, I wondered, did Uncle Tate see? Gramma had mulled for weeks, no doubt, before offering to go with him to worship among strangers. It had probably taken all the courage she could muster to volunteer, for his sake. And now this.

"Have you been invited out to dinner somewhere, Tate?" Mama asked.

"Yes, I have." His look dared her to comment further.

"Well, you're a grown man and what you do is your own business," Gramma said, not doing a very good job of hiding her feelings. "But I wish you'd told me before I cooked so much food for Sunday dinner."

"There's not but one of me, Ma," he said. "The rest of you have to eat."

In all his time here, he hadn't caught on that our meals without him were mere skeletons of those that were set before him. When he excused himself to go change his spattered shirt, the three of us sat on in silence, looking questions at each other.

Finally Gramma leaned toward Mama and whispered, "Ruth, do you think he's seeing some woman?"

"I think he might be," Mama whispered back.

Uncle Tate seeing someone? What kind of desperate woman must she be?

"Close your mouth, Missy," Mama said, "unless you have something you want to say."

I closed my mouth, but then I opened it again. "Who?"

"We could ask him," Mama said.

Gramma straightened and pursed her lips. "Certainly not! If he doesn't want to tell, that's his business." Then she added, "But I don't know why he has to be so sneaky about it. Not unless he's got a guilty conscience."

Uncle Tate's footsteps coming along the hallway ended our conversation for the time being. He'd changed the shirt and added a coat and tie.

"I'll be going now," he announced in a louder than necessary voice.

"It's only nine-fifteen," Gramma pointed out. "You'll get to Foursquare before anybody else does."

"That'll give me a little extra time to study and meditate," he said.

"Then if I were you, I wouldn't forget my Bible," she commented with a sniff.

Uncle Tate looked down at his empty hands and reddened for the second time that morning. "I knew there was something," he mumbled, retracing his steps. When he came back through the kitchen clutching his Bible and Sunday School Quarterly, he scowled so fiercely that Gramma didn't even ask when he'd be home, although I'm sure it was on the tip of her tongue.

A little while later, we were on our way to Sandy Hill, me squeezed into the backseat of the VW, Mama and Gramma up front. I daydreamed, vaguely aware that Mama carried on a one-sided conversation to which Gramma responded in monosyllables. Her face was stern under the black felt hat.

We passed Alma Dean's place. In the un-treed yard, the house shone yellow as butter in the morning sun. The

AYDEE'S SHORT CUTS sign hung unmoving in the still, cold air. Gramma pressed her bony knuckles against the window as a way of pointing at it.

"I bet *she's* still in bed," she said, her words dripping judgment.

"She works late on Saturday nights," Mama said. "Lots of people come in after work. Sometimes it's nearly midnight before the last customer leaves."

"She ought to go to church once in a while," Gramma said. "It breaks her mother's heart."

"Maybe she would if people wouldn't talk about her behind her back," Mama said pointedly.

We drove on. I thought about Alma Dean taking her time on Sunday morning, drinking a second cup of coffee, reading the newspaper. She was a free woman, no doubt about it. Maybe Alma Dean was the person I needed to talk to. She had no stake in my future. I could count on her being up front with me. She would ask hard questions. She, better than anyone else around here, could predict outcomes, given certain choices. I remembered how angry she'd made me the night she cut my hair, but I knew now it was because she saw through me, saw even the part I'd hidden from myself.

Suddenly, Gramma burst out, "I just hope it's not one of those Foursquare women!"

Startled out of my musing, I sat up and leaned forward, the better to hear over the noise of the engine.

"Now, Ma, we don't have any idea," Mama said.

"I don't know who else it could be," Gramma grumbled, looking out the window.

I thought she was probably right. Foursquare had been Uncle Tate's only social life since Aunt Mary died. I tried to picture the mystery woman. She'd probably be a pasty-looking person with heavy eyebrows and lots of dark hair who wore high-necked, long-sleeved dresses. She'd be religious and meek. What if he married her and brought her to the house to live? No wonder Gramma was upset.

The steeple of Sandy Hill church poked up through the trees, the first thing a traveller on the road might see. Like our house, the church is a glaring white, to suggest purity, I suppose. In the summer among green trees, it looks like a picture postcard, but in winter when the grass is dead brown and the trees bald, the scene is stark and less forgiving. I thought about Mama coming back here after her so-called disgrace. It must have been pretty awful, especially after Grampa had made such a to-do about it in front of the whole congregation.

I had a hard time keeping my mind on churchly matters. Jim sat beside me with his arm draped over the back of the pew and his hand doing things to my upper arm that Gramma wouldn't approve of.

I could see Jim and me occupying this same pew for years to come, with maybe some kids on each side of us. I looked around the congregation and saw plenty of families that had started and grown up exactly like that—high school sweethearts marrying, settling right here. They seemed happy and content. Next week this time, I could be on my way home from Moriah College, or I could be sitting right here in this same place. I didn't know which it would be. Jim invited me to come home with him for dinner, but I declined. My nerves were raggedy enough without the loud teasing and boisterousness of the entire Perkins family.

By contrast, dinner at our house was like a funeral meal, although Mama and I tried to keep up a steady conversation. Gramma had no interest in either the preparation or serving. Not having Uncle Tate there to eat was like being an actor performing to an empty auditorium. More than that, his mystery life had her stumped and worried. Not that she came right out and said so, of course.

After we cleaned up the kitchen, Mama headed upstairs for a nap. I settled down in Grampa's easy chair—which had become Uncle Tate's—to read a novel I'd been saving for after exams.

"You needn't get too comfortable," Gramma said. "When Tate gets home, he'll want to sit there and take a nap."

"Yes'm. I'll move when he comes."

Minutes ticked by. Cars passed on the highway. "That might be him," she said every now and then, listening hard. Then, "No, I guess not."

Most Sunday afternoons, Gramma went with Mrs. Lula Burrell to visit shut-ins, but today of all days, Miss Lula's arthritis was acting up. Gramma didn't drive, but if she could, I had no doubt she'd be tooling up and down the roads looking for Uncle Tate's truck under the guise of visiting. After an hour or so of trying to ignore her fidgets, I offered to take her anywhere she'd like to go.

"No," she said, lifting her chin. "I'm fine." She got up

from her chair for the umpteenth time to go look out the window.

I put down my book. "I need some exercise—I think I'll ride my bike. Are you sure you don't need a ride somewhere?"

She hesitated for a fraction of a second, but then she said no again. I was relieved. I was going to see Alma Dean. I couldn't telephone her without Gramma listening in on the conversation, so I decided to take my chances on catching her at home. I went out to the shed and unlocked my bike from the post, feeling like an escaping prisoner.

I pedalled hard with my head up, facing the wind, full of purpose. In my mind, Alma Dean loomed like some kind of palm reader. By sundown today, I would know what to do.

I signalled a right turn for the car behind me and turned into Alma Dean's yard, my opening remarks already prepared. The first thing I saw was Uncle Tate's truck parked beside the yellow house.

I took a sharp breath and squeezed the handbrake. The bike stopped so suddenly I almost flipped over the handlebars. The tires made skid marks in the brown grass.

I got off the bike, but I didn't let go of the handlebars. I needed something to hold on to while I thought what to do next. I searched for reasonable explanations. There were none. Unisex hairstyling is not the In thing in Tucker, and besides, I knew that Alma Dean wasn't open for business on Sunday. Nothing in my experience of either Uncle Tate or Alma Dean pointed toward this strange turn of events. What were they doing in there? If I went up and knocked on the door, how long would it take for Alma Dean to answer? Would Uncle Tate try to escape unnoticed out the back way?

It occurred to me that he wasn't exactly hiding. The pickup was right out there where anyone who drove by could see it. Maybe he didn't care if anyone knew he was there. That, in itself, was a revelation.

My common sense began to take over. Uncle Tate would not easily forgive what would appear to him to be spying, and I didn't want Alma Dean to think of me as just one more of Tucker's gossips. I mounted the bike and left the way I came, but I pedalled slowly to delay the return home as long as possible. I was sure my face would reveal what I knew, whether I told it or not.

The highway was busy with Sunday afternoon traffic. I did my white-line balancing act, lifting my hand in greeting when drivers tooted their horns at me, but my mind was elsewhere. I thought about Uncle Tate and Alma Dean Slater Rodriguez. I marvelled in the same way a person might who is viewing a real camel or a giraffe up close for the first time, not really sure I saw what I thought I saw. From somewhere behind me a horn blew, then I heard a familiar sputtering that could only be Uncle Tate's truck.

I hunched over and sped up, moving as far to the edge of the road as I could without actually getting off on the muddy shoulder. I waited for him to pass me by, but he didn't. The sputtering slowed and he crept along behind me, honking the horn. A car zipped past us going in the opposite direction, barely missing another trying to get around Uncle Tate. I feared that we would cause a traffic pileup right out there in the middle of nowhere.

I made sure the way was clear and signalled to him that I was turning around. I wheeled to the opposite side of the highway and made a winding motion with my hand and arm so he would roll down the window.

"What do you want?" I asked peevishly, to cover up my anxiety.

"Put your bike in the truck and I'll give you a ride the rest of the way."

His pleasant manner had the effect on me of a stun gun. Had he seen me through the window at AyDee's? I unlocked the tailgate and shoved my bike into the truck bed. I slammed the tailgate shut and tramped around to the muddy side. He had already opened the door for me.

"I never thought to see you out here this time of day," he said, as I climbed in and fastened the seat belt. His coat was folded properly on the seat beside him. There was no sign of his tie. He stepped on the gas and we zoomed up the road, coming closer and closer to home.

"I just saw your truck at Alma Dean's," I said casually, watching to see his reaction.

His head jerked around and his eyes narrowed. I waited for a blast of accusing words, but nothing happened. He turned his eyes back to the road and swallowed. Then he said, "Oh. Well?"

It sounded like he was asking me what I thought. But I chose to interpret it another way. "Well, I could ask you what you were doing over there, but it wouldn't be any of my business."

"No, it wouldn't."

We were within sight of the house. "I thought *you* thought she was an agent of the devil," I said.

Uncle Tate cleared his throat. He took a deep breath and said, "I was wrong about that."

I thought maybe it was time for the Second Coming. In my lifetime, I had never heard Uncle Tate admit to being wrong about anything. We were almost to our bridge, but he wasn't slowing down for the turn. I braced my feet against the floorboard, expecting to be slung against the door, but he went right on by.

"We just passed the house," I said.

"*I* know that! I'm not ready to go in there yet. I have to think."

We sputtered on up the road, one mile, two miles. We passed the Perkins's house. Jim's truck was parked under the big oak tree in front.

"You and Jim pretty serious?"

The question was totally unexpected and not particularly welcome. I thought Uncle Tate was trying to turn attention from his own situation.

"That," I said, "is my business."

"You don't have to bite my head off," he said. He was so mellow I wondered if Alma Dean had drugged him or something. I had a hard time imagining the two of them loving up on each other. The mere idea was embarrassing.

There were things I wanted to know, such as when they started seeing each other and how it had affected his re-

180

ligion, but I had shut the door in my own face by not answering his question about Jim and me.

"Yes, we are," I said, "but you were wrong at first. Three weeks ago, there was nothing going on between us."

"I believe you," he said, talking to me as though we were the same age, as though I might have as much sense as he did. "Something like that can come up on you from behind. Hit you right over the head unbeknownst."

I wasn't sure I liked for us to be lumped in the same category as Uncle Tate and Alma Dean, but I couldn't help how he saw it. I made a bold move.

"How'd you make up for what you said to her that night you came to get me? I don't see how she let you into her yard again, much less—" I let it drop, not wanting to spell out the rest.

"She is not vengeful," he said. "A remarkable woman."

His awe of her was unmistakable. Clearly, Alma Dean had conquered. But what could she possibly see in Uncle Tate? My opinion of her had altered during the past hour, or at least it had become confused. I sighed inwardly, aware for the first time how much I'd been counting on my conversation with her. Now I doubted it would ever take place.

By this time, he had gone a good ten miles past home. I glanced at my watch. It was getting late in the afternoon and I remembered the state Gramma was in when I left the house.

"Well," I said, "you'd better turn around and head back. The longer you wait, the harder it's going to be."

Chapter 18

The new semester began Tuesday morning. On the chalk-board in English class was the following quotation:

> *In this world there are only two tragedies.*
> *One is not getting what one wants, and the*
> *other is getting it.*
>
> —OSCAR WILDE, FROM
> *LADY WINDERMERE'S FAN*

I wondered whether it was just a coincidence that Ms. Pope had chosen these particular words as the Quote for the Week. Sometimes I've pictured her, Mrs. Arnot, Mr. Francis, Señora Smith, Mr. Preston, and Ms. Hollins huddled around the coffee table in the smoke-filled teacher's lounge discussing my situation, but I know that's a self-centered, not to say paranoid, way of looking at things.

Coming back to the routine of school was a relief after the turmoil of the weekend. Uncle Tate's bombshell admission that he was seeing Alma Dean had the predictable effect. Mama shrieked, then leaped up and grabbed him around the neck, laughing the whole time. It was the first I'd ever seen her hug Uncle Tate for fun. Gramma drew in her breath and frowned.

"Just how serious is this, Tate?" she demanded.

"Well, I don't know how to answer that, Ma," he said, struggling to maintain his dignity. "I've not been out with any woman since I met Mary twenty-six years ago."

"I mean," Gramma said impatiently, "do you intend to marry her?"

"Ma, for goodness sakes!" Mama spoke up. "Just seeing somebody doesn't mean you've got to marry them."

Uncle Tate's smile was sheepish. I guess he never thought to see the day when he'd have Mama for an ally instead of an enemy.

Gramma was not comforted. I guess she thought he had made a permanent life decision when he sold his and Aunt Mary's house and came to live at the homeplace. Maybe it had never crossed her mind before today that he might get married again and crowd up the house with a new daughter-in-law. I wanted to remind her that at least Alma Dean wasn't a Foursquare woman, but it seemed too early in the game to make that point.

Since then, the tension in our household has thickened to the consistency of axle grease. Gramma acts like she's been left on an ice floe to die, while Uncle Tate blunders about, unintentionally rubbing salt into the wound with such remarks as "Alma Dean cooks the best meat loaf I ever ate!" Mama believes that Uncle Tate is more smitten by Alma Dean than vice versa, which restores my faith in Alma Dean's common sense.

It has dawned on me that in almost every romance with which I am personally acquainted, there is some obstacle to happiness. In the sixth grade, we made a mock Egyptian frieze on butcher paper that stretched the length of one wall. Every Egyptian on that frieze was staring at the back of the head of the person next to him or her. It was like each one had an eye on someone . . . or something . . . better and didn't seem to appreciate the attention they were getting from behind. Even though the frieze ended at the corner of the room, you could imagine the line going on and on for as far as the eye could see.

Mrs. Pope began introducing the material for the new nine weeks, but I couldn't get the quotation out of my mind. If a person took it seriously, the only way to avoid tragedy was by not ever wanting anything. There was no hope for people like me who wanted at least two things and couldn't choose between them.

Ms. Hollins had sent word for me to come by her office at the beginning of lunch period. As soon as the bell rang, I hurried downstairs, aware that Jim would probably be waiting for me in the cafeteria.

The door to Ms. Hollins's office stood wide open. She sat at her desk eating something from a Tupperware bowl and looking like royalty in a purple sweater. Her hair was pulled up in a sleek bun. She lifted her hand and beckoned me in, pointing to the chair.

184

"Have some salad?" she offered, pushing the bowl toward me.

"No, thanks. I have my sandwich. Jim's waiting for me in the cafeteria."

Her eyebrows arched. "You two looked sharp at the dance," she said.

I smiled and thanked her. I guess I hoped she'd say more, maybe comment on what she thought about the two of us together.

Instead, she asked, "Are you nervous about Saturday?"

"Well, yes . . . sort of." The truth was I wasn't letting myself think about it at all.

"Who's going with you to Harborough?"

"I'm going by myself," I said.

If she wondered why Jim wasn't going, she didn't ask. Although I longed for his company, I couldn't see putting him through two days of waiting around for me in a strange place, especially when everything I was there to do was designed to pull me away.

"Well, you'll do fine. I have a map of Harborough right here, and I've already marked the route so you can go straight to the campus." She pulled the map out of a drawer and laid it on the desk with a brisk pat.

"Now, in terms of what to expect," she went on, "you'll be well taken care of once you get there. A student will be assigned to you so that you won't have to fret about knowing where to go or what to do next."

"*If* I get there," I said, trying to laugh, but it sounded more like a choke. "What if I get lost?"

"Missy, you will *not* get lost." She said it like an order

which I was to obey or else. I nodded, listening hard after that, afraid I'd miss an important detail.

"I can't tell you exactly what questions you'll be asked, but most interview committees want to know how well you keep up with current issues. They'll ask your opinion. Don't bluff if you have no idea what they're talking about. Say you don't know and wait for the next question."

My heart had begun to pound, exactly as if I were already in the middle of the interview. Ms. Hollins put the top on her empty bowl. I thought she was through with me, but when I said my thanks and started to get up, she said, "Wait. I have one more thing to say."

I sat there, tense.

"Missy, these are copycat times—everybody's trying to look and act and be like somebody they've seen on TV. In all the time I've known you, you never have. You'll do fine. You'll do *better* than fine."

She pushed away from the desk and stood up then, and I did, too. "Come by here before you leave school Friday. I have a little something for you to take along on the trip."

"What is it?" I asked, but she just smiled. She handed me the map and I tucked it in the back pocket of my jeans. I thanked her and told her I'd see her Friday afternoon, but as I headed for the cafeteria, I felt only confusion.

I finally spotted Jim among the bodies alone at a table on the far side.

"Gosh, I'm glad you didn't leave!" I fell into the chair beside him, breathless from my illegal sprint down the hall. "I had to see Ms. Hollins."

186

"It's okay," he said. "Melanie was here till a minute ago."

"Oh?" I was careful, waiting. "What did she want?" I pulled out my sandwich and unwrapped it, for something to do.

"She came to apologize for how she acted Friday night—says she hopes we can be friends." He watched me as he spoke, as though testing the words for credibility.

"Did she mean just you or all of us?"

"I don't know."

"What did you say?"

"I asked her what did she mean by 'friends,' " he said. "She got mad and went off in a huff."

Expansive with relief, I gave him a big smile. I was not so dumb as to believe Melanie would settle for friendship, especially if I went off to college next fall.

If.

It kept coming out like that. Never *when*.

I'd eaten about half the sandwich when I realized how unusually quiet Jim was. He'd finished his lunch and now he drummed his fingers on the table and looked out over the cafeteria instead of at me.

"Something wrong?" I asked.

"Not life or death," he answered. "But you aren't going to like it."

"Tell me." I smiled again, to show him I could take anything.

"I flunked the English exam," he said.

"You *what?*" It came out before I could grab it back, not just the words but my dismay and disappointment as well.

187

"I knew you'd be mad," he said.

"Jim, *why?* I helped you study. We went over everything. What happened?"

"I guess I just don't remember things as good as you do," he said. "I got all the names mixed up. I'd've probably done better if I hadn't studied so much."

"Does that mean you flunked for the semester?"

"Looks like it. Ms. Pope says I better work my tail off this semester to pass for the year."

"You have to pass English to graduate."

"I don't really care if I do," he said. "What difference will it make out there in the boat whether I passed English, or got a piece of paper that says I graduated?"

"That doesn't sound like you, Jim," I said. "With only one semester left, not finishing would be like starting to haul in a full net and then, right before getting it to the boat, letting all the fish drop back into the water."

I was impressed with my own analogy. I expected him to see my point.

"I guess you'd have a hard time explaining to your college friends a boyfriend who flunked out of high school, huh?" he said.

I could only stare at him.

"Look, nothing like that ever crossed my mind. It hurts my feelings that you'd think so."

He lifted his hand then, as a signal he didn't want to talk about it anymore. But the damage was done. When the bell rang for class, we didn't even walk as far as the cafeteria door together.

188

Chapter 19

Mama was the only family member up when I came downstairs with my suitcase, ready to leave. She had cooked breakfast for me, but the very smell was enough to give me the heaves.

"Don't worry about it," she said, when she saw my despairing face. "I think I fixed breakfast more to make me feel good than for you."

"I really appreciate it." I eyed the mountain of scrambled eggs. "I wish I could eat it."

Mama smiled gently. She came over to the chair and gave me a hug, resting her cheek against my hair. "Oh, honey, I wish I could do this for you."

"Wouldn't you be scared?"

"Of course I would!" She laughed a little. "But being scared never killed anybody. Sometimes it helps a little."

I thought about Mama doing what I was getting ready to do and managed a smile, so she wouldn't worry about me. I kept up the front, even when she walked with me, out into the morning dark, to the car. She gave my shoulders one last squeeze before I got in and fastened my seat belt.

"Drive carefully, now," she said, hugging her bare arms close to her chest. "Call me at the store if there's any problem."

"I'll see you tomorrow afternoon," I said, letting my mind skip over the possibility of any problem.

I drove west alone in the dark. Barring accidents or car trouble, I would be at Moriah College by ten o'clock. My first interview would be at two, my second at three-thirty.

Last night Jim took me to Elizabeth City to dinner. We dressed up and everything. He said it was to wish me luck. He said he knew I was going to win.

But he didn't say he hoped I would.

We talked and talked. I tried to explain that how I felt about him had nothing to do with whether he passed English or graduated from high school. I told him I worried about his future, but I could tell by that flat look in his eyes that he just didn't buy it. His good-night kiss was quick, like he didn't want to put too much feeling in it.

Last night was a tumble of dreams and wakefulness that left me worn out, torn up. I dreamed that people were pulling at me and I couldn't get away.

I thought back to the day when I brought the Financial Aid Form home. It seemed to me that up until then, I was in charge. Since then, everybody had gotten into the act.

Where are you when I need you, Bill Cord?

The unexpected question nearly bulldozed me off the road. What a dumb question! Bill Cord was never around when anybody needed him. I'd lived my whole life making sure *I* wouldn't.

It was scary in a way, like he had somehow managed to edge his invisible self into the VW. I made myself look sideways, to be sure nobody was there.

No *body*. But something. What did he . . . it . . . want to say to me?

I gripped the steering wheel, feeling stony and stubborn, but at the same time curious.

You can throw the fight.

My heart thumped so hard, I actually took my right hand off the wheel and laid it on my chest, like I thought that would calm me down.

Throw the fight?

Sure. Don't try so hard. Somebody's got to lose. Why can't it be you?

I looked out at the flat, brown land and tasted the answer. That would at least buy me some time.

In Rocky Mount, I stopped at McDonald's for a Dr. Pepper and a bathroom break. I spread my North Carolina map on the table in front of me and studied it once again, tracing with my finger the inked-in lines put there by Ms. Hollins. I should follow the beltway around Harborough all the way to the west side, then take the Valley Street exit ramp. It would take me straight to Moriah, to the front entrance, which Ms. Hollins said was a great stone arch with Latin words chiselled across the top. You can't miss it, she told me. But I knew I could. I pictured myself riding on and on to the end of Valley Street and beyond, never finding the stone archway at all.

I was only making matters worse. I folded the map, took one last swig of my drink, and went back out to the VW. Maybe it wouldn't start. It had been known not to at crucial times. I turned the key, almost hoping for a dying chug, but the engine started right up. Within five minutes, I was out of Rocky Mount. The sign said seventy-something miles to Harborough.

Even though it was Saturday, there was more traffic than I was used to. Steering two-handed, I counted the exits around the beltway, aware of cars and trucks zooming by on either side of me, hoping I wouldn't get in the way of anyone in a major hurry. Finally a sign loomed. VALLEY STREET EXIT 1 MI. I edged into the right lane and in a short while, I was tooling down the curving ramp toward Valley Street. I counted the cross streets and suddenly, to my left, I saw the stone archway and the low stone wall that enclosed the campus.

Moriah's campus was like a haven in more ways than one. Within the busy city, it was a quiet enclosure of spacious rolling lawns and enormous oaks, like a royal park. Even in winter, with the grass brown and dry, it looked gracious and orderly. Maple trees arched over the long front drive like a cathedral roof. I knew from looking at the catalogue that the buildings were laid out in a large double quadrangle, and that the domed one in the middle was the administration building, Landon Hall. Someone would meet me there.

I had no trouble finding a parking place in front of a VISITORS sign. I turned off the engine and sat, breathing deeply.

I took stock, holding my hands out to see if they were shaking, inspecting the pleated skirt for wrinkles. The rear-view mirror showed a pale-faced, somber-looking girl who might be going to a funeral. I chewed on my lips to ripen their color. I practiced a smile. It looked more like a grimace. I opened the purse Alma Dean had loaned me and took out the piece of paper on which I had scribbled all Ms. Hollins's instructions. My panic level soared and I quickly stuffed it back into the purse.

I had to find a bathroom. I opened the door and unfolded from the car. On the backseat lay Ms. Hollins's coat with a fur collar. This is what she had for me when I went by her office yesterday afternoon. "It's just a loan," she had said when I started to protest. "It'll make you feel good. I know."

The cold dry air seeped through my sweater and I put on the coat. The soft fur brushed my neck and cheeks like a friendly cat. Traces of Ms. Hollins's perfume lingered in it. I had to admit that the coat's elegance did things for my spirits. I straightened my shoulders and lifted my chin.

When I pushed my way through the double glass doors of Landon Hall, I found myself in a large round chamber with a maroon-carpeted stairway winding up, up out of sight toward the skylight dome. The floors were marble. Voices and footsteps echoed like notes at the end of a song. A woman in a brown suit smiled at me in a friendly way.

"Are you one of our scholarship finalists?" she asked.

"Yes, ma'am." I took my hand out of the satin-lined pocket and grasped the one she offered. "I'm Melissa Cord."

I hadn't called myself Melissa in my whole life, except when someone needed to know my real name. I wondered if the coat made me do it.

"I'm Dean Brooks," the woman said. She had a sharp but kindly face, which she kept at an upward tilt. "We're so happy to have you. Let me introduce you to your hostess for the weekend."

She turned and, queenlike, lifted her right hand in the air, beckoning to someone. I looked beyond her to the leather-covered bench beside the far wall to see a person about my height rise to her feet and head in our direction. She didn't look frilly or made-up. She could be me, I thought.

"Leigh Morrison, this is Melissa Cord," Dean Brooks introduced us. "Melissa, Leigh is a junior and one of our scholarship holders. She went through this process three years ago, so she can tell you anything you need to know."

Leigh and I smiled at each other. "Hello," she said. "I hear you're from Tucker."

"Yes," I answered. "You probably don't know where that is."

"I guess I *do*. I'm from Manteo."

My smile stretched into a grin. I could feel it move up to my eyes. "Well, I'll be!" I said.

"Come on." Leigh took me by the arm. "We'll get you

194

settled, then I'll bring you back here to meet some of the others."

I was happy to be under her wing. We drove the VW around to the back of Leigh's dorm, then took my suitcase upstairs to her room on the third floor. I didn't feel self-conscious with her. The hall smelled perfumed and musty. Noteboards, cartoons, posters, and cutouts decorated the doors of each room, announcing the personalities behind them.

"My roomie's gone home for the weekend," Leigh said, as she unlocked the door to the room and stood aside for me to enter.

The room was a little larger than mine at home, but it seemed crowded with posters on the wall, stuffed animals on the bed, refrigerator, hot plate, and two-of-everything pieces of furniture. Leigh told me that I'd be on the bottom bunk, which I was glad to hear, not wanting to distinguish myself first thing by rolling off the bed into thin air during the night. She showed me where to hang my clothes, and pointed to the bathroom between this room and the next. I thought about all the years I'd had a room of my own and wondered if I would ever be able to share a space with someone else, especially someone I didn't know.

Thirty minutes later, we were on our way back to Landon Hall. I clutched a schedule that told me what I'd be doing for the next twenty-four hours.

"Try not to worry about the interviews," Leigh said. "You'll be talking to faculty—department heads mostly, and they're all as nice as can be."

"Oh, I don't doubt that." I sighed. "Only, there's so much I don't know."

"Well, sure," she said with a chuckle. "If you knew everything, you wouldn't need to come here, would you?"

I remembered her words that afternoon as I sat at a long gleaming table with the interviewers, a mixture of men and women. I hoped I'd be able to remember their names.

"Melissa Cord," one of the professors said, reading my name off the paper in front of him. His name was Dr. Floyd and he looked like somebody's grampa with white hair and beard. His shoulders stooped; his suit was a size too large.

I sat up straight and licked my lips, getting ready.

"I see that you work in a day-care center," he said, peering down the table at me.

"Yes, sir. Since ninth grade."

"Do you find that there's a greater need for day-care in your area of the state than the community is able to provide for?"

I thought of Perry and his tired little mother who could barely scrape together the money it took to keep him at our center, and I was off and running. There were the Clayton twins whose parents work in Elizabeth City and who had both been in day care since they were six weeks old.

I had been lucky to have Gramma and Grampa while Mama worked. Gramma taught me my letters and numbers. Grampa taught me how to use tools. Mama read to me every night. But most of the kids in our center depended on us to be the readers and the teachers. We had too many children for the number of helpers, and some of us were not really qualified.

I realized suddenly that I was rattling on. I closed my mouth and looked around. I saw one or two amused expressions. My face burned.

"Are you interested perhaps in a career in early childhood education?" asked Dr. Salton. She was the head of Moriah's Department of Education.

"I . . . yes," I said with a certainty that took me by surprise. The truth came to me like a burst of light. I felt as though the wind had been knocked out of me. I wanted to quit answering questions right then and go away to think. Maybe I had just gotten carried away. Maybe tomorrow I wouldn't feel the same.

But they asked about other topics—the Middle East, censorship, affirmative action. At some point, I realized that I was enjoying the interview. Before I knew it, my time was up. I was almost sorry, but I was also relieved.

When I walked out of the conference room into the waiting area, I saw the anxious faces of the others who had not yet been in.

"Look," I said, "don't worry. It's fun."

They looked at me in utter disbelief, almost with hatred, and putting myself in their place, I understood.

I headed for the nearest bathroom. It wasn't until I looked at my elated self in the mirror that I remembered I had intended to throw the fight.

The second interview was more personal. This time, alumnae joined some different faculty members. Why did I want to come to Moriah, a women's college? If I won a scholarship, would I be willing to devote some time to helping recruit other scholars in the years to come? What campus activities appealed to me most? What did I want out of life?

In this session, I tried saying "Early Childhood Education," liking the confidence it gave me. It was what I wanted to do. I felt like another person now, in another life. I had seen on a bulletin board in the hallway that a well-known author would be on campus next week to read and visit classes. A famous violinist would give a concert in the auditorium of the music building. The governor would appear two weeks from now to present his views on education for the next century. Where I came from, you read about events like this in the paper or saw news clips on TV. But here is where they happened.

By late afternoon I was exhausted. Leigh offered to show me other campus sights before dinner, but I told her I needed to be by myself for a while. She pointed me in the direction of the pond at the west end of the campus and I headed toward it, fur collar turned up against the February wind. The sun was low in the sky, shining above and behind the huge oaks that dotted the landscape. Already I loved this campus—its orderliness, its beauty, the richness I knew was there waiting to be uncovered.

At the water's edge, I brushed off a stone bench and sat down. The pond's green surface rippled in the wind. The reflections of the surrounding trees scattered fragments of light and shadow. I thought of Cedar Bay, the Sound, the ocean. When I came here to school, this little bit of water would be all I had to remind me of them.

Not if. When. Because now I knew that whether or not I won the big scholarship, this is where I wanted to be.

The wind died down a little. I felt myself relaxing, accepting. I tried to picture Jim beside me, but it didn't work. In so many ways, we were like two parts of the same person, but our walking-around lives just didn't fit together. He would see the change in me when I returned home tomorrow. He would know what I had decided, and even though we had the rest of the school year and the summer together, when autumn came, we'd do what we had to do.

It was nearly time for me to meet the others for dinner. I got up from the bench and walked to the edge of the pond, bending way over to look down into it. I saw the reflection of my head and shoulders silhouetted by the sky's light. No features, just an outline, like a shadow. In my mind, I filled in what I could not see. I smiled and imagined I saw the reflection smile, too.